"I'm here about my daughter. I want to ask…" Jordan stopped midsentence and turned to leave.

Felicity stood still, her face very pale. "You owe me an explanation," she said. "You can't come here in the middle of the night and not tell me why."

He shrugged. "It doesn't matter."

"What is it? What's wrong? Is it little Mandy?"

Jordan almost wanted to plead, but his pride wouldn't let him. "Mandy's miserable, we need you—would you say yes if I offered you your old job back?"

Grace Green grew up in Scotland but later emigrated to Canada with her husband and children. They settled in "Beautiful Super Natural B.C." and Grace now lives in a house just minutes from ocean, beaches, mountains and rain forest. She makes no secret of her favorite occupation—her bumper sticker reads: I'd Rather Be Writing Romance! Grace also enjoys walking the seawall, gardening, getting together with other authors…and watching her characters come to life, because she knows that once they do, they will take over and write her stories for her.

Grace Green loves to write deeply emotional stories with compelling characters. She's also a great believer in creating happy-ever-after endings that are certain to bring a tear to your eye!

Jordan's sister has her own story in
The Pregnancy Plan #3714
Harlequin Romance® on sale August 2002

Books by Grace Green

HARLEQUIN ROMANCE®
3622—THE BABY PROJECT
3658—TWINS INCLUDED!

THE NANNY'S SECRET

Grace Green

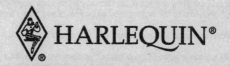

HARLEQUIN®

TORONTO • NEW YORK • LONDON
AMSTERDAM • PARIS • SYDNEY • HAMBURG
STOCKHOLM • ATHENS • TOKYO • MILAN • MADRID
PRAGUE • WARSAW • BUDAPEST • AUCKLAND

For John

ISBN 0-373-03706-6

THE NANNY'S SECRET

First North American Publication 2002.

Copyright © 2002 by Grace Green.

This edition published by arrangement with Harlequin Books S.A.

® and TM are trademarks of the publisher. Trademarks indicated with
® are registered in the United States Patent and Trademark Office, the
Canadian Trade Marks Office and in other countries.

Visit us at www.eHarlequin.com

Printed in U.S.A.

CHAPTER ONE

FELICITY FAIRFAX'S gray eyes pricked with tears as she gazed into the window of West Vancouver's Kiddi Togs store. "Wouldn't Mandy look adorable in that daffodil-yellow dress, Joanne? Oh, I'd love to buy it for her. If only—"

"If only Jordan Maxwell would let you anywhere near his daughter. But that," Joanne declared, "is never going to happen."

"How can he be so cruel?" Heart aching, Felicity turned to her friend, her heavy blond braid glinting in the early June sunshine as she flicked it back over her shoulder. "Yes, his wife and my brother Denny had an affair, but that had nothing whatsoever to do with me!"

"Of course it didn't. But you're a Fairfax and that's enough for Mr. High and Mighty Maxwell. As far as he's concerned you're persona non grata...and will be for ever." In an obvious effort to divert her, Joanne indicated a quilt displayed in the window. "Is that *another* of yours?"

"Mmm."

"I love the kitty motif. And I'm impressed. You've really upped your output lately!"

"I've had lots of time to sew now that I don't have Mandy to look after." Felicity clutched her friend's hand. "I miss her desperately, Jo. I've cared for her since she was a week old and I've always loved her as

5

if she were my own. My life feels so empty, so pointless, now."

"I know, sweetie…but you must try not to dwell on it." Gently, Joanne eased her away from the window. "Let's go treat ourselves to a latte and a chocolate biscotti and talk about something else."

"I can't even *think* about anything else."

But Felicity allowed herself to be led along the sidewalk toward the Hill o' Beans café on the corner.

"Jo," she fretted, "I worry about her. I know her mother didn't pay her much attention, but even so, for Mandy to have lost both of us in one fell swoop…she must feel utterly abandoned and must be missing us terribly."

"Missing *you*, at any rate—you're the one she spent most of her days with for the past almost four years. Jordan Maxwell must be either incredibly stupid or incredibly stone-hearted to have cut you out of her life."

"I hear he's enrolled her at the Wedgwood Avenue Day Care."

"Really? It has a terrific reputation and wonderful staff. She'll be happy there."

They'd reached the Hill o' Beans, and as they entered the café with its tantalizing aroma of freshly ground coffee beans, Joanne added, a little anxiously, "Don't you think?"

"I hope so." With a deep and soul-felt sigh, Felicity followed Jo to the counter. "Oh, I certainly do hope so."

Jordan Maxwell swung open the door of the Morningstar Realty office building and strode into the umber-carpeted foyer.

"Good morning, Jordan." The middle-aged recep-
tionist grimaced. "The meeting's already started."

He was late. Again. His boss was going to be hopping
mad. If Phil Morningstar had one obsession, it was punc-
tuality. The world of real estate waited for no one! And
every morning this past week, since enrolling Mandy at
the Wedgwood Avenue Day Care before returning to
work after a prolonged absence, Jordan had been late for
Phil's daily finger-on-the-pulse meetings.

"Thanks, Bette, I'll prepare myself for the usual flack
attack. So...did you apply for that raise yet?"

"Not today I haven't. His ulcer's playing up."

"Oh, great, just what I want to hear!"

"Jordan, just a second, you've got a—"

"Later, Bette." He loped past the reception desk.

"But—"

He shook his head, and rounding the corner to the
corridor, headed toward the boardroom. As he went, he
scraped an exploratory hand over his jaw...and muttered
under his breath as he felt the unevenly bristled skin.

He should've taken the few extra minutes to shave at
home. He'd never mastered the art of running an electric
razor over his chin while driving—and trying to shave
while dodging his way through rush-hour traffic and at
the same time trying to pacify Mandy who was wailing
her heart out in the passenger seat beside him was nerve-
shattering at best.

The boardroom door was ajar, and he could hear
Morningstar's abrasive voice all the way along the corridor. But when he pushed the door open, a hush fell
over the room.

Jordan felt a dozen pairs of eyes fixed on him, but his
own came up against Phil Morningstar's steely glare.

"Sorry, Phil. I got held up." He slipped into his seat, the rustle of his suit jacket against the polished mahogany table the only sound in the room.

Then somebody chuckled.

Dumping his briefcase on the floor, Jordan glanced around the table, and saw his colleagues were smiling. Jack LaRoque, the office Lothario, grinned and, focusing his gaze on the breast pocket of Jordan's jacket, tapped his own.

Jordan looked down and saw Mandy's pink hairbrush sticking out of his pocket. He must have stuffed it there after tidying her mop of blond curls. His gaze shot back to his boss, whose lips were compressed to a pencil-thin line.

"Sorry," Jordan muttered. But as he thrust the brush into his briefcase, his cell phone rang. Cursing silently, he checked the caller ID.

"I'll have to take this." He threw Phil an apologetic glance. "It's my daughter's day care."

The caller was Greta Gladstone, the owner.

"You'll have to come and pick Mandy up," she said. "She's been having hysterics ever since you dropped her off. This isn't going to work out, Mr. Maxwell. You'll have to come up with some other arrangement."

His day was going rapidly from bad to impossible.

"I'll be there," he said, "in five minutes."

He surged to his feet. "Phil, I'm sorry, I have to—"

"You took three months off to be with your daughter after you lost your wife, Maxwell. Fine. Understandable. But enough is enough." Morningstar pressed a hand to his chest and belched. "I'll give you one more week. Get your personal problems sorted out before next Monday or—"

"Next Monday. Right. Thanks, Phil." Jordan was already halfway out the door. "Thanks a bunch. I'll have everything sorted out by then. I swear."

Jordan called his sister the moment he got Mandy home.

"Lacey, thank the lord you're there." His daughter had fallen asleep in the car, and he held her limp figure in his arms as he spoke. "I need you to come up. Are you free?"

Lacey was twenty-five to his thirty-four and a world-famous model. She was forever flying off somewhere to a shoot; and she routinely smiled or pouted at him from the cover of top fashion magazines when he passed the local newsstands. With hair like sable, skin like cream, and legs that didn't know when to stop, she was drop-dead gorgeous.

She was also super-smart, and he was hoping she would come up with some way out of his present dilemma.

She lived just a few minutes away, in a waterfront condo, and by the time he heard her car purr up his drive, he'd made a pot of coffee. As he was walking across the foyer to the sitting room with two steaming mugs, Lacey let herself in by the front door with her own set of keys.

"How come you're at home?" she asked. Lending elegance to a simple white cotton T-shirt and blue jeans, she preceded him into the sitting room, walking with the trademark fluid glide that had graced hundreds of catwalks. "Shouldn't you be out selling houses, now that Mandy's at the Wedgwood Avenue Day Care?"

"Sit down, Lace." He waited till she'd arranged her long willowy body in an armchair, before he handed her one of the mugs. Setting his own mug down on a side table, he paced the room. "Mandy's not at day care. She's upstairs, asleep."

"Is she sick?"

He shook his head.

"Then wh—"

"She was *expelled*." He scratched a despairing hand through his hair.

"Oh, honey." Lacey rested her mug on her knee. "She wouldn't stop crying?"

"Yeah, she's been the same all week. When I made to drop her off today, she was sobbing and clinging to me like a terrified kitten. I felt like a monster, prying her little fingers free and then handing her over...as if I didn't want her." He squeezed his eyes shut for a moment, to try to blot out the ugly image. When he opened them again, he saw worry clouding his sister's face.

"Oh, Jordan, I'm so sorry."

"What the hell am I going to do?" he asked. "If this goes on, she's not the only one who's going to be thrown out. Morningstar's had it up to here with me. I may be one of the top salesmen in the Lower Mainland but he's given me till a week Monday to get my personal affairs in order and if I haven't, it's—" He slashed his throat with his index finger. "Game over."

He slumped down in a chair and somber silence fell on the room as they drank their coffee.

When they'd finished, Lacey said in a tentative tone, "Honey, won't you even consider Fel—"

"No!" He shot up from his chair and scowled down at her. "Don't even say that name in here, I don't want—"

"We're not talking about what *you* want now." Lacey stood and confronted him, her green eyes pleading.

"Jordan, I understand how you feel—after what happened, I don't blame you for hating Denny Fairfax—"

"Lacey, I'm warning you—"

"But his sister had no part in what he did, she didn't even *know* until after the car accident that he and Marla had been involved in an affair for several months before it happened. And although you lost your wife—"

"In more ways than one!"

"—Felicity Fairfax didn't come out of the whole mess unscathed. She lost her *brother*—or as good as lost him. According to all reports, he's never going to come out of that coma. And, honey, Felicity and Mandy adored each other. I *saw* them together, it was beautiful. Won't you at least *consider* rehiring her? You wouldn't even have to see her—at least, not too much, only when you dropped Mandy off as Marla used to, and then pick her up again at night—"

A heart-rending wail coiled its way down the stairs and into the sitting room.

Jordan blew out a sigh. "She's awake," he said. "Let's see what you make of her."

They went upstairs and into her bedroom, which opened off the landing. The child was still crying.

Jordan felt a sense of panic as he and Lacey crossed to the crib. The situation was escalating out of his control. If this continued, he'd lose his job and then how would he support himself and his daughter? He'd made a helluva lot of money over the years but Marla had spent it as fast as he could earn it—sometimes even faster.

"Poor little mite." Lacey bent over the crib rail, but Mandy wasn't aware of her because her eyes were tightly shut. She was lying on her back, her cheeks wet and flushed scarlet as she wailed at the pitch of her voice.

Lacey waited till her niece stopped to catch her breath, and then she said, "Hi, sweetie, what's the matter?"

Mandy froze, and then gulping back a choking sob, opened her eyes. When she saw Lacey, she started crying again, harder than ever, and rolling over she pressed her face to the pillow, so that her cries were muffled.

Jordan leaned over and lifted her up into his arms. Holding her close, he murmured soft words, and in a while, she stopped crying and just clung to him, shaking and giving an occasional gulping sob, her arms clamped around his neck.

Lacey ran a hand down her niece's back, lightly. "Sweetie—"

Mandy jerked away from her caress. And tightening her grip around her father's neck, started to sob again.

"I thought," Lacey whispered to Jordan, "that you'd have managed to get her to sleep in her bed again by this time. She won't give up the crib?"

He shook his head. "No way. It's a lost cause. Look, you may as well go. I shouldn't have had you come over, wasting your time. There's nothing you can do, nothing anyone can do. This is one problem that doesn't have a solution."

Lacey opened her mouth to speak. But thought better of it when she saw the forbidding frown that warned her not to bring up Felicity Fairfax's name again.

"Thanks for coming over," he said. "I do appreciate it, Lace."

"You're welcome, big brother."

She gave him a hug and walked over to the door. But when she reached it she paused. And just before she disappeared around the corner, she said, in a rush, over her shoulder, "There is a solution to your problem, Jordan, and you know very well what it is!"

Felicity wrapped her lavender and pink floral-patterned china teapot in bubble wrap and tucked it carefully into the packing box. Then straightening, she smiled when she noticed RJ batting a wad of tissue with his paw.

Some people said cats sensed when a move was afoot and became twitchy and unsettled. Not RJ. Felicity had been cleaning out her apartment and packing her belongings ever since she'd recently sold the street-level property and RJ was exactly as he always had been: playful and inquisitive and supreme monarch of all he surveyed.

Felicity moved over to the kitchen sink and washed her hands. "We'll be leaving here for good, on Monday, RJ. What do you think of that?"

He ignored her.

"We're going over to Vancouver Island, to stay with Mom until I find a place of my own. I might even be able to afford a little rancher, one with a tree in the garden because I know you love to climb!"

Oblivious to the prospect, RJ leaped up into the air before pouncing down on the scrap of paper as if it were a mouse.

"Moving to the island will be for the best." Felicity tried to smile, but catching sight of her pale taut features in the chrome surface of the kettle she gave up the attempt. She really had nothing to smile about anyway. But surely, once she was back on the island with her family for support, she would eventually find joy in her life again?

But no matter how hard she tried to convince herself, she knew in her heart she would never get over losing Mandy.

RJ had grown bored with his paper, and scampering over to Felicity, wound his fluffy silver-white body sinuously around her right ankle.

She dipped down and picked him up. As he clutched her knit top, she stroked him, wondering if she'd ever felt quite so desolate. "It's not as if I'm likely to ever have a baby of my own, RJ," she murmured. "I'm twenty-seven, time's running out, and still no sign of Mr. Right."

If RJ could have spoken, she mused, he might have reminded her she'd had no fewer than three serious proposals of marriage over the years, but she'd turned them all down.

"Because I wasn't in love!" she protested. "I enjoyed their company, but not one of them made me feel the way I want to feel…"

RJ purred loudly, as if to ask, "And what way is that?"

"The way it is in romance novels." Felicity's voice was dreamy. "I want my heart to ache for him when we're apart, I want it to sing when we're together, I want to feel as if I'm on Cloud Nine when he takes me in his arms, I want to feel as if I'm drowning when he looks into my eyes. Wherever he is, that's where I want to be—"

The shrill ringing of the wall phone made her jump—and RJ leaped from her arms. Stepping around the packing boxes, she lifted the receiver. "Hello?"

She sensed someone at the other end of the line, but no one spoke.

"Hello?" she repeated. "Who is this?"

Still no reply.

"Who are you trying to—"

At the other end, the phone crashed down.

"Well!" She took the receiver from her ear and stared at it indignantly, "you might at least have said, 'Sorry, wrong number!'"

Jordan slumped back in his swivel chair and stared grimly at the phone on his desk. He'd been gearing up for days to make the call and when push came to shove, he couldn't go through with it. He could not, he *would* not, have anything to do with Denny Fairfax's sister—

"What happened? Did you make the call?"

He jerked up his head and saw his sister in the study doorway. "I thought you were upstairs with Mandy."

"She's asleep. Finally." Lacey came into the room. "So...did you make the call?"

"Yeah."

"You talked to Felicity?"

"No."

"Did you leave a message on her answering machine?"

"No."

"Why didn't you? Why didn't you just ask her to call you back when she gets home—"

"She's home."

"She's screening her calls? How can you know that?"

"No, she's not screening her calls. She picked up the phone."

"I don't underst—oh." Lacey slid her hip onto the edge of the desk, and sent him a disappointed reproachful look. "You didn't have the courage to—"

"It had nothing to do with courage, dammit." He pushed to his feet and planting his fists on his hips he glowered at his sister. "It had to do with—"

"Bitterness." Lacey gave a sympathetic nod. "Jordan, we've been over this ground before. OK, you feel bitter. But you're letting your emotions get in the way of what's best for your daughter. Mandy loved Felicity Fairfax, and it's my belief that she's missing her dreadfully and that's why she's so difficult to handle. She's letting you—and everybody else!—know that she hates the way things are now and she wants to get back to her old routine, where she felt safe, and loved, and happy. Jordan—"

Lacey's beeper went, and she exhaled a weary breath. "Honey, I have to go. I have a plane to catch tonight. Will you promise me you'll phone again…and *talk* to her this time? I do realize there's a possibility she may not even want to take on the job. She may blame Marla for what happened to her brother, and may feel as bitterly toward the Maxwell family as you do toward hers!"

"So what you're saying now is that I should call and plead with her to look after Mandy again and risk having her spit the suggestion back in my face?"

"That's a chance you'll have to take."

He walked Lacey to the front door. The night was clear and bright, and from this location high on the slopes of West Vancouver, he could see the city lights spread out ahead like an endless field of stars…

Heaven upside down.

Lacey put her arms around him and gave him an encouraging hug. "Do it, Jordan. For Mandy's sake."

*   *   *

Felicity continued packing till well after midnight then decided to call a halt. After dragging the boxes she'd packed through to the utility room next to the kitchen, she let RJ outside for a quick prowl and then got ready for bed.

She'd just put on a T-shirt nightie, braided her hair, and slathered her face with white cleansing cream, when through the bathroom window she heard RJ yowling to get in.

She hurried to open the back door before he disturbed the neighbours.

"Come in, you handsome beast—" Her breath froze in her throat. RJ shot past her while she stood rooted to the spot and stared, startled out of her wits, at sight of a man standing on her doorstep. With the moon at his back, his face was in shadow, but his hair was dark and his eyes glittered as they fixed on her.

"If that's the way," he drawled, "that you welcome strangers in the night, I've come to the wrong place."

What did he mean?

Uh-oh. *Come in, you handsome beast.*

Feeling like a fool, she nevertheless felt her fright dissipate. If he'd meant to harm her, surely he'd have grabbed her by now. Still, she stepped quickly back and pulled the door till it was almost closed, and peered at him through the narrow gap left.

"What can I do for you?" she asked. "Are you lost?"

His chuckle had a harsh quality. "No, I'm not lost," he said. "At least, not in the way you mean."

"What do you want then?"

"I want to talk to you."

Felicity frowned. "Who are you?"

Impatiently, he looked around, and as he did, his profile was outlined against the bright backdrop of the moonlit sky. A sharply cut profile, with a swathe of dark hair falling over his brow, a strong nose, an uncompromising chin.

Fantastic bone structure. The kind that artists would adore. And women, too...

Felicity blinked the thought away.

"I'm going to close the door right now," she said, "If you don't tell me who you are and why you're here."

He turned and faced her. Just then, the people upstairs put on their bedroom light, and the yellow rays shone down on this stranger, illuminating him.

He *was* a handsome beast, Felicity thought. Handsome—and hostile. Oh, yes, no doubt about it...hostile.

"I'm Jordan Maxwell." The words came out as jarringly as a jackhammer on granite. "And what I want to talk to you about is not something I wish to discuss out here." He shoved his hands into his pockets and lanced her with his glittering gaze. "Aren't you going to invite me in?"

He had expected someone who looked older. More solid. More mature.

Not this slip of a thing in an old T-shirt nightie, with her hair in a braid and her eyes filled with apprehension.

When she'd invited him in, it had been with an unsure gesture of her hand. The only words she'd spoken since had been to ask him if he wanted a drink.

He'd have liked a Scotch; she offered tea.

While the kettle was boiling, she'd left the room. When she came back, her face was scrubbed clean and she'd put on a gray cotton shortie robe and a pair of thongs.

So here they were, sitting at her kitchen table, drinking tea that tasted like cranberries.

And still she hadn't said a word.

She looked down at the table as she sipped her tea, so he had an opportunity to scrutinize her further. She didn't resemble her brother. She was fair, he'd been dark. She was slim as a reed, he'd been ruggedly built...and had looked mature. But he'd been anything but. He'd been irresponsible and wild and spendthrift. Just like Marla.

They had been a pair.

He felt anger rise inside him as it did so readily these days. But he controlled it.

"I'm here about Mandy." He shoved aside his half-empty mug. "I want to ask—" He broke off as his glance moved beyond her to another room. A utility room. He could see packing boxes there, all neatly taped up. At the same time, he belatedly realized the kitchen had an echoing feel to it. And the walls were bare, many of the shelves empty.

"Are you *moving?*" He stared at her.

"Yes. I'm going home."

"Where's home?"

"The island."

It was the last thing he'd expected. Oh, he'd known she might turn down his proposal outright and that even if she'd accepted it, she might haggle about salary, hours, any number of other things. What he hadn't once anticipated was that she might be leaving the Lower Mainland and going to live on Vancouver Island. "You've made your plans?"

"Everything's settled. I'm going to stay with my mother till I find a place of my own." She finished her tea, put down her mug. "Now…it's very late…and you still haven't told me why you're here."

"It doesn't matter. Not now." He rose from the table, put his mug on the counter. "I'll be on my way."

He was at the door, opening it, before she said, "Wait."

He turned. She was standing still, her face very pale.

"You owe me an explanation," she said. "You can't come here in the middle of the night and not tell me why."

He shrugged. "You won't be here, so…what I wanted to ask you…doesn't matter."

"It was something about Mandy, wasn't it? If there's anything I can help with, please let me know. I realize it must be difficult for you to look after her—she has her own little ways, and if it'll make it any easier for you, I'd be happy to sit down and go over them with you. For example, her hair gets tangled after it's washed, and to keep her from fussing when you brush it, you have to…"

Her voice trailed away when she saw him drag a weary hand over his nape.

"What is it?" She took an urgent step toward him. "What's wrong? You *must* tell me!"

"Mandy's miserable. I've never seen a kid so unhappy." Jordan wanted to go down on his knees and plead with her to stay but his pride wouldn't let him. Instead, he gave another shrug—a deliberately careless shrug. "I just thought—at least, my sister Lacey suggested it, I was dead against the idea—Lacey suggested it might help if I were to offer you your old job back. For Mandy's sake.''

Her lips parted in a round, soundless. ''Oh.''

''But since you're leaving, I'll have to find someone else. It's no big deal.'' He turned his back on her and opened the door. ''I shouldn't have bothered you.''

He went out into the night and as he walked in the moonlight to his car, he felt as if the world and all its worries were pressing down on him from every side.

What the *hell* was he going to do now! He'd told Ms. Fairfax he'd find someone else.

There *was* no one else.

He kicked at a stone, and hissed out a word that would have made Lacey's hair stand on end.

Wrenching open the car door, he was about to throw himself inside, when from behind him he heard someone call, ''Mr. Maxwell! Wait!''

And when he turned around, Felicity Fairfax was running breathlessly toward him.

CHAPTER TWO

FELICITY thought her heart was going to burst.

What Jordan had said had stunned her. And then joy had exploded inside her, lending wings to her feet as she raced out of the apartment.

Now, catching up to him, she gasped, "Do you really mean it? You want me to look after Mandy again?"

"I don't recall using exactly those words...but yes, that's what I came here to ask."

"In the middle of the night?"

"I was hoping you could start tomorrow. I'd planned—if you were available—to bring Mandy over here on my way to the office. But since you're moving out of the area—"

"But I don't have to move—I don't *want* to move! If you could only wait till I find another place, there's nothing in the world that I'd like more than to look after Mandy again."

A car stopped, farther along the street. Its headlights illuminated Jordan's face, and there was no mistaking his expression of relief. Then the vehicle turned into a driveway and once again his face was shadowed.

"I can't wait," he said. "I need you to start tomorrow."

"But I have the movers coming on Tuesday. And I'll have to find another place to live—"

"You'll stay at Deerhaven."

"At *your* house?"

"Right." Impatience snapped in his voice. "You'll come home with me now, and tomorrow you can change all your moving arrangements."

Felicity felt her initial exultation give way to indignation. If he thought he could ride rough-shod over her, he had another think coming.

"I have not," she snapped back, "even finished packing yet!"

"You can do that tomorrow night after I get home from work." Restlessly, he shoved his hands in his pockets, to a jangling of keys or coins. "Now, if that's all settled, I'll give you a couple of minutes to pack a case with your immediate needs, and then we can—"

"I have a cat."

"Ah, yes." His tone was mocking. "The handsome beast. I'm not a cat lover myself. I don't suppose you'd consider giving him up for adoption?"

"I most certainly would not!"

"Then he'll be part of the package. Just keep him out of my way, or I won't answer for the consequences." He leaned back against the car. "Right, I'll wait here." He made a big play of looking at his watch. "I'll give you twenty minutes to get ready."

Felicity took thirty.

Oh, she was ready in twenty, but she sat in her darkened bedroom for an extra ten, letting her new employer cool his elegant heels outside.

Jordan was well aware that Felicity Fairfax had saved his job for him. And he knew he should be grateful to her. But as he drove his car up the narrow drive leading to his house, all he could feel was resentment—resentment that Fate had put him in the position of being *beholden* to her.

It made his blood boil.

Had Fate not dealt him a bad enough hand already, throwing his wife and Denny Fairfax together at that charity "do" last Christmas? His wife had always been an outrageous flirt, but at least she'd known which side her very expensive bread was buttered on and so she'd never become involved with anyone outside of their marriage...until she'd met Denny Fairfax—

"Who's looking after Mandy just now?" Felicity asked.

He pulled to a halt in front of the house. "My sister. I believe you've met her."

"Lacey. Yes, she came to pick up Mandy several times. Couldn't *she* look after Mandy tomorrow?"

"No." He could have told her Lacey was flying off to California in the morning; he chose not to. Felicity Fairfax was going to be his employee and he wanted to keep their relationship as impersonal as possible. "Now let's get inside."

He carried her case in from the car, she carried a holdall in one hand and the cat in a wire cage in the other.

As he opened the front door, Lacey came across the hall from the sitting room. Before she realized he wasn't alone, she said, eagerly, "How did it go?"

He stood aside to let Felicity step past him, and she walked into the hallway, swinging the cage in front of her.

"Oh, Felicity!" Lacey beamed at her. "I'm so pleased!"

"Hi, Lacey." Felicity returned the friendly smile. "It's lovely to see you again."

"And is that your case? You're going to stay here? Oh, I guess so," she chuckled, looking at the cat. "You've moved your family with you." She crouched down and said, "Psst! RJ!" The cat pulled back, pushing its rear end against the cage. Lacey laughed, and straightened. "It's so good of you to come, Felicity."

Jordan cleared his throat. "Is Mandy still asleep?"

"Yes. She's been a bit unsettled but she hasn't wakened since you left." Lacey gave Felicity another friendly smile. "I'm leaving now—I have an early start tomorrow, I'm off to California on a shoot." She swept up her scarlet linen jacket from the deacon's bench at the door, and swung it over her shoulders. "I'll be able to leave with an easy mind, knowing Mandy's in your hands."

"Thank you, Lacey."

"'Bye, Jordan." Lacey gave him her usual hug. "I'll be in touch when I get back. Probably Friday."

As the front door clicked shut behind her, Jordan said, "I'll put you in the room next to Mandy's so you'll be able to hear her at night."

They walked up the stairs and as they did, he saw her looking around.

"I can't think why," she said, slowly, "But I feel as if I've been here before. It all looks so familiar to me—those Mandori oil paintings, the cream marble floor in the hall, this lapis-blue carpet on the stairs and…this." She ran a hand lightly over the Benducci grandfather clock in the curve of the stairwell. "Where have I seen this before? I know it's one of a kind, made for some Italian count…"

"Do you read architectural magazines?"

"My friend Joanne sometimes passes her copy on to me."

He ushered her on, up to the landing. "Then that is where you may have seen the interior of Deerhaven. There was a spread in—"

He paused as they reached the door to Mandy's room. They'd spoken quietly, but they must have disturbed her because she'd started to fret. She sounded as if she might be waking up, though her mumbles and whimpers were drowsy.

Felicity had paused beside him. He heard her breathing quicken. "May I see her?" she asked.

"Best not go in. She'll drop off again."

But she wasn't about to drop off again. He heard the creak of her mattress, and pictured her scrambling to her feet. He almost groaned aloud. Another sleepless night lay ahead, not that there was much of the night left.

Now she was crying, the cries becoming louder, more demanding, by the moment. This time, he did groan aloud. He loved his daughter more than anything on this earth, but so help him, if she didn't let him get some sleep, he was liable to go take a very long walk off a very short pier—

Felicity touched his forearm lightly. "Why don't you show me where I'm to sleep, and then get yourself off to bed. I'll take care of Mandy."

"No, I'll need to show you the lie of the land. Downstairs, too, because I'll be out of here before you're up in the morning. I need to give you a tour—"

"I'll find my own way around." She swung the cat cage forward. "Is my room along this way?"

She was bossing him. Taking charge.

Well, okay, but just for tonight. And just because he

was bushed. Tomorrow, he'd show her who was head honcho around here.

Fighting a huge yawn, he opened the door next to Mandy's.

"There you are," he said. "It's all yours. En suite included." Mandy's crying had taken on a shrill singsong note, which he knew from experience she could keep up for hours.

"Good night, Jordan." Felicity walked past him and set down the cat's cage.

He knew he should say 'Thanks' but the word stuck in his throat. He turned to go…and then turned back.

"What about the cat?" he asked curtly.

"RJ? Oh, he'll be fine now till morning. Then I'll take him for a walk outside—on a leash—to get him acclimatized to his new surroundings." She dropped her holdall on the carpet. "In a few days, once I'm sure he's not going to run away, I'll give him free rein."

Even as she was speaking, she'd tossed her shoulderbag on a chair and thrown her anorak onto the bed.

Flicking back her braid, she looked at him with a challenging sparkle in her eyes. "I'm ready," she said. "You can hit the hay now, and I'll see you…" She gave a light shrug, her gaze amused. "Whenever."

She walked past him again and headed for Mandy's room. After a brief hesitation, he turned on his heel and proceeded along the corridor in the other direction, to his own room, which was on the far side of hers.

Halfway there, he turned to glance back…

She had already disappeared from view.

Felicity tiptoed into the child's bedroom.

Rose-pink light glowed from a night-bulb plugged

into an outlet by the curtained window. In its gentle gleam she could see a single bed to her right. It was neatly made but unoccupied.

She flicked her glance around and was taken aback to see Mandy in her crib—the large white-painted designer crib Marla Maxwell had delivered to Felicity's apartment when Mandy was six months old. It had remained at Felicity's apartment until Jordan Maxwell had sent a van for it the day after his lawyer had notified Felicity her services would no longer be required. That was three months ago, right after the car accident that had changed all their lives.

Felicity had known that although Mandy had loved napping in her crib when she was at the apartment, she had long since graduated to sleeping in a bed when she was at home. So why on earth was the three-year-old not in that bed now? Certainly the crib was big enough for her because she was dainty as an elf, but surely using it was a backward step? She'd have to ask Jordan about it tomorrow.

Tonight, her aim was to comfort his daughter.

Mandy was standing up, hanging on to the crib rail, her head thrown back, tears spilling from her eyes. She was crying in a keening way that tore at Felicity's heart.

Tears pricking her own eyes, she whispered, "Oh, my poor darling!" as she hurried across the carpeted floor.

She ached to scoop Mandy up in her arms, but she didn't want to frighten her. Instead, she gently set her own hands atop the child's small-boned fingers, which were wrapped tightly around the top rail, and in a soft and soothing voice, she started singing Mandy's favorite lullaby.

The crying stopped.

Mandy froze. And for a long moment, the only sound was a sudden loud hiccup that echoed around the room.

Then slowly, very slowly, she lifted her head up from its lolled-back position, and stared, wary-eyed and open-mouthed, at Felicity.

Felicity smiled. And blinked back a tear.

"Hi, sweetheart," she whispered. "It's me."

Another hiccup. Then a shaky, teary voice that was filled with wonderment and disbelief. *"Fizzy?"*

Felicity's smile was watery. "Oh, yes, my darling, darling child. It's Fizzy. Come to look after you."

Now she leaned in and tenderly lifted the three-year-old in her arms, and cuddled her against her bosom. Mandy seemed lighter, even more fragile than she'd been last time she'd held her. Poor baby, she'd been through so much.

Feeling a surge of joy as the child's slender arms wound their way around her neck, Felicity sought the nearest chair—a comfortable armchair by the hearth—and sank down.

"Fizzy?"

"Yes, sweetheart." Felicity smoothed a hand over the tear-damp hair, and kissed the tear-damp forehead. "What is it, my little love?"

"I missed you." Mandy started to weep again, but this time in low-strained sobs even more heartbreaking than her loudest most desperate wails had been. "I missed you every day."

"And I missed you, too, precious. You'll never know just how much. But we'll always be together, from this moment on. You can count on it."

She felt the grip around her neck tighten as the child gulped out an anguished "Promise, Fizzy?"

"Yes, my darling." Felicity injected all the assurance she could into her words. "I promise."

If there was one thing he hated, it was the smell of burned toast.

It hailed Jordan as he strolled along the corridor to the kitchen next morning, and set his teeth on edge.

She wasn't to have known, of course, that toast always stuck in that old toaster; a person had to stand beside it and pop the toast up when it looked ready. Still, she shouldn't even have been downstairs, far less making toast! She should have had the savvy to stay upstairs till after he'd gone. She must know how he felt about her; and the last thing he'd want was to have to make conversation with Denny Fairfax's sister at the best of times...and first thing in the morning, before he'd even had his first mug of coffee, was certainly not that.

Surly, and prepared to be curt, though not to the point of rudeness, because dammit, he needed her—at least for the time being!—he shoved the kitchen door open.

And found the room empty.

Oh, she'd been down all right, and not too long ago. The smell of burned toast was even more cloying in here. The sweetish aroma of strawberry tea fought a losing battle for survival under it.

A black-and-red tea caddy, with a pattern of dragons, sat on the counter.

A note on the table read "Your Toaster's Broken."

And over by the back door, on the gleaming white-tiled floor, her cat was throwing up.

"Good morning, Jordan!" Bette welcomed him with a cheery smile. "Glad to see you back...and you're the first one in!'' She ran an approving glance over him. ''Looking like your old self, too. Nice shave, hair immaculate, no pink hairbrushes peeking out of your pocket! So I gather you've solved your problems with Mandy? You've found someone reliable? You're—''

''Yes, yes...and yes, to whatever your third question was going to be.'' Jordan ran frustrated fingers through his hair, making a mockery of Bette's ''immaculate'' comment. ''Java, Bette. Please tell me you've made the coffee?''

She raised her eyebrows. ''Yes, I have. But you don't usually have any here till midmorning. You always have coffee at home first thing in the morning to set you up—''

''Not this morning, I didn't!'' He was already halfway to the staff room. Over his shoulder, he threw back, ''Not with that darned cat throwing up all over the place.''

The coffeepot was full. He took his mug from the cupboard—the one he'd got last Christmas from Mandy with her picture on it. According to the child, ''Fizzy'' had had it done at a photo shop, 'specially for him.

He'd never met ''Fizzy,'' his daughter's baby-sitter, but he'd appreciated the thought that had gone into the gift. He'd always meant to let her know, but time had slipped away from him...and then...it was too late. The very name ''Fairfax'' had become anathema to him, and ''Fizzy'' Fairfax was the last person in the world with whom he'd wanted to become involved in any way, shape or form—

''Cat?'' Bette materialized at his side. ''You can't *stand* cats! What was a cat doing in your kitchen?''

Jordan filled his mug with coffee. "You don't want to know."

"But I do."

Bette Winslow had been married four times, and had, she often said, "Seen it all." In her early fifties, she had the kind of personality that invited confidences—and all the agents knew that Bette in Reception was closer than a clam.

Jordan was a private person and normally he didn't talk to outsiders about his personal problems. Today, however, frustration had him wanting to tell someone about his impossible situation. And if anyone would listen and show him sympathy, it would surely be Bette.

He added milk to his coffee, and drank half of the teeming mug in one long swallow.

Only then did he set the mug on the table, fold his arms over his chest, and say, "It's Felicity Fairfax's cat."

Like everyone else in the office, Bette had learned that his wife and Denny Fairfax had been having an ongoing affair during the several months before Denny had smashed up his sports car, killing Marla in the process and sending himself into a coma. And she must know how he would feel about any of the Fairfaxes.

"So," she said, "you've rehired Felicity Fairfax to baby-sit Mandy, and she's going to live in."

Bette, he mused, never needed to have things spelled out. "Right," he said.

"A wise decision."

"I had no other choice. My hours are erratic, you know I work late more often than not, and I couldn't go leaving Mandy with her while I'm closing some late-night sale or—"

"I meant it was a wise decision to rehire Felicity Fairfax. I don't know her, but my cousin Joanne does, and she has only the nicest things to say about her."

"You missed my point, Bette. It wasn't a so-called 'wise decision' to rehire the woman. A Fairfax is the last person I'd have hired, if I'd had a choice. I hadn't."

"You're not telling me, Jordan Maxwell, that you're tarring the sister with the same brush you were quite justified in tarring her brother with!" Censure tinged Bette's voice. "For heaven's sake, Jordan, the girl—"

"She's not a *girl!*" He felt like a schoolboy put out after being reprimanded by a favorite teacher. "She's a woman, and one I don't want to be around." He *sounded,* now, like a sulky schoolboy, and that irritated him.

"You have to put *Mandy* first. She's the one who's important here...not you. The poor child lost not only her mother but the baby-sitter she loved. I know she adores you but she needs a mother—or at least, a female to mother her. I don't think you'd have had quite so serious a problem with her if she'd lost just *one* care-giver—in that case, she'd have been able to turn to the other for comfort."

"I know that," he growled. "You don't have to..." His voice trailed away as a thought occurred to him.

"Then what are you going to do, Jordan? I don't see a way out. You're determined to do what's best for Mandy, but you're just as determined to dislike this woman. Children sense conflict. It's the last thing Mandy needs."

"Don't worry." Jordan put his hand in the small of Bette's back and ushered her toward the door. "What you said just now...you've given me an idea." Smiling, he escorted her through to the reception area. "Thanks to you, I believe I see a way out of my dilemma."

Felicity looked down at her sleeping charge and wondered if she'd ever felt happier. She'd told Joanne the truth when she'd said she couldn't have loved Mandy more if she were her own child. Being here, caring for her again, was the most wonderful thing that had ever happened to her.

Her heart went all mushy now as she gazed upon the little girl, who looked adorable in sleep. Her bubbly blond curls were tousled, her cheeks were flushed to the same pink as her nightie, and her rosebud mouth pouted, as if she were blowing bubbles in her dreams.

She looked like a fairy...but at the thought, Felicity frowned, wondering again why Jordan still put her to bed in her crib. She reminded herself to ask him about it.

In the meantime, she was looking forward to spending the day with Mandy and wished she would wake up!

As if the child had read her mind, she opened her eyes and when she saw Felicity, her face split in a smile.

She scrambled to her feet. "Fizzy! You're still here!"

"Of course I'm here, darling. Didn't I tell you I always would be?"

"Let me out! Out, out, out!"

Laughing, Felicity unhooked the side of the crib and slid it down. Then taking both Mandy's hands, she encouraged the child to jump, and swung her down, her narrow feet landing with a light thump on the carpet.

"I've been waiting for you to waken," Felicity said, "so we can start our first day here together."

Ten minutes later, they were on their way downstairs,

with Mandy wearing the yellow T-shirt and shorts she'd chosen from her wardrobe, with a pair of yellow sandals.

"After breakfast," Felicity said, "We'll go out for a walk. But before we go out, would you like to show me over the whole house? It's lovely, but so big. I'm sure to get lost if you don't show me where everything is."

"And I'll show you outside, too." Mandy skipped along happily. "There's a garden, and a greenhouse, and a hot tub. Daddy sometimes uses the hot tub, but only in the winter. He says it's for grown-ups, to relax after a hard day. Do you have hard days, Fizzy?"

She'd had some very hard days over the last three months, but now, thanks to whichever angel was sitting on her shoulder, life was going to be wonderful.

"From today on," she said, "for me...and for you, Mandy dear...the hard days are over."

Jordan didn't get home till after seven.

Silence met him as he walked into the foyer. He stood and listened. Not a sound...except for the steady tick-tock of the grandfather clock in the stairwell—a clock he personally thought looked hideous. The price had also been hideous, but Marla had wanted it so Marla had bought it.

He pushed the memory away.

With his linen jacket slung over his arm, he tugged the knot of his tie loose and made for the stairs. Ascending with barely a sound, he reflected that it was a very long time since he'd sensed peace in the place.

And it was peace he needed.

First day back on the job, he'd scrambled to catch up—contacting clients, checking new listings, dealing with an irate couple whose newly purchased condo had sprung a leak just days after they took possession...

He would shower, go down to the kitchen and rustle up a sandwich. And he'd take it—along with a beer— to the lounge, where he'd put up his feet and read the newspaper. Thank the Lord the Fairfax woman was keeping out of his way. He saw, when he reached the landing, that her bedroom door was closed. With a bit of luck, he mused, she was in there and would stay there.

The cat, he hoped, was in there, too.

Mandy's door was half open, the heavy curtains closed, the night-light on.

He moved the door gently in, and tiptoed to the crib.

She was sound asleep; he could hear her soft breathing.

He leaned over and with a tender hand, touched her fine curly hair.

"Good night, princess," he whispered. "Daddy loves you, and things are going to be much better from now on. Just don't go getting too attached to your precious Fizzy again, because I'm going to ease her out of here as soon as I can find someone else to look after you. But don't worry, honey, I'll do it in such a way you'll never even notice she's gone."

He stood there a while longer, thinking, listening to her breathe, mulling over his plan.

And then, after blowing her one last little kiss, he turned on his heel and walked out of the room.

"What an absolute *snake!*"

Shooting up to a sitting position in Mandy's single bed, Felicity hissed out the words as she stared, outraged, at his back and the closing door.

Because Mandy hadn't wanted her to leave after she'd been put down in her crib for the night, Felicity had offered to stay with her till she slept, and had lain on the bed.

But she had fallen asleep herself.

She'd wakened when she'd sensed someone in the room. She'd been drowsy at first, but had come fully awake when she'd heard Jordan Maxwell warn his sleeping daughter not to get too attached to her "precious Fizzy again"—because he was planning to get rid of her.

Well, she wasn't about to be got rid of.

And forewarned was forearmed.

But what could he have in store for her?

What was his devious plan?

Whatever it was, she'd better get out of Mandy's room right now in case he came back.

She snuck across the room, peeked out to ensure the coast was clear, and then dashed to her own room.

Once she closed the door, she could hear the sound of water running nearby. His bedroom must be next to hers. Had he just come home? If so, he was probably taking a shower before going down for his evening meal.

She waited, with her ears pricked, and a short while later she heard his bedroom door open. Taking in a deep breath, she opened her own door and casually stepped out.

She almost bumped into him.

"Oh!" She gave him a fake-surprised smile. "You're home! Your dinner's in the oven, Jordan. Shepherd's pie, I hope you like it. I'll come down with you, and tell you all about the lovely day Mandy and I have had."

CHAPTER THREE

FELICITY FAIRFAX was the last person he wanted to chat to…if he happened to be in a chatty mood, which he most definitely was not!

But of course he did want to know how Mandy had been.

"Fine." His tone was gruff, his manner abrupt as he took off across the landing…with *her* at his heels. "You can talk while I make myself a snack."

"I said I'd made shepherd's—"

"I don't want you cooking for me." He bounded down the stairs…but she stuck to him like a shadow. "I'm used to looking after myself."

"Mandy says you fired your housekeeper after your—"

"I've never liked strangers around the place." There, that should knock some of the pep out of her. "When I come home from the office, the last thing I want is to have to make small talk with—"

"That's *you*. But what about Mandy? Who's been making her meals for the past three months?"

"I have." He leaped down the last few steps in one bound.

She scuttled down after him. "You can cook?"

His heels clicked on the marble foyer as he crossed to the kitchen corridor. The lighter, dainty click of her sandals irritated him. "Sufficiently well to keep us from starving."

He slid the kitchen door open and stood back to let her enter first. As he followed, he was so taken up with the delicious savoury aroma in the air, he almost tripped over the cat which suddenly scooted out from under the table.

"Sorry," she said. And obviously sensing his displeasure, added, "I'll pop him down to the laundry room."

"Can't you just put the beast outside?"

"He needs a few days to get his bearings, take over his new territory, before I can give him that freedom. He'd probably rocket away and then not be able to find his way back...and it would break my heart to lose him."

Break her heart to lose a *cat?* What kind of a heart did the woman have, that it could be broken so easily!

She went out into the corridor with the mewing animal. He heard her open the door to the basement, then heard her clattering down the basement's wooden stairs.

He turned to the fridge.

The mouth-watering aroma drifting from the oven seemed to intensify by the moment. Trying to ignore it, he poked about in the fridge and took out a head of lettuce, a large tomato, a wedge of cheddar cheese, and a jar of mayonnaise, and set them on the counter along with a bottle of beer.

Then he reached into the bread bin for the loaf he'd bought at the deli two days ago...and came up with nothing.

What the—

"Are you looking for bread?" The tinkling voice came from behind him. "Mandy loves bread pudding so I—"

He turned to face her. "So you…?"

"I made some. And I'm afraid I used up the last of your loaf. I'd noticed the freezer in the basement, and I just assumed you'd have more loaves down there, but…" She spread out her hands in a "How was I to know?" gesture. "I can pick up some bread and rolls when I go out tonight."

"You're going out?"

"I have to finish my packing," she reminded him. "The movers will be coming in tomorrow."

"How are you going to get over there? I can't drive you, can't leave Mandy—"

"A friend's coming to pick me up, after I call."

"Why don't you phone her now?"

"It's a him, not a her. OK, I'll do that. He lives in the area so he'll be here in a few minutes, I'll just have time to fill you in on Mandy's day." She whirled around, made for the wall phone and picked up the handset.

She made the arrangements, and finished by saying, "Come to the back door, Hugh. I'll be in the kitchen."

After putting the phone down, she took the shepherd's pie from the oven, and set the steaming dish on the island. Next she brought out a smaller casserole. Removing its lid, she revealed piping-hot, chunky-cut carrots and green peas.

Before he could say, "Thanks, but I'll just make myself a salad," she spoke first.

"Mandy is so sweet!" She scooped a generous helping of shepherd's pie onto a plate. "She gave me a tour of the house and grounds." Adding vegetables to the plate, she prattled on about how much they'd both enjoyed their day, as she set the plate in front of him. "Now what else do you need? Oh, salt and pepper—"

"Miss Fairfax, you and I have to talk. I—"

"Call me Felicity." She gestured toward the table. "Don't stand there, sit down and eat your dinner. Here," she commandeered his bottle of beer, "let me."

Before he could stop her, she'd taken an opener from the cutlery drawer and levered off the cap. Then she set the bottle and a dimpled glass beer mug on the table.

"There," she said. "I think that's everything. Sorry there aren't any buns or bread. As I said, I'll get some when I'm out."

Jordan felt as if he were being rolled over by a runaway train—and he snatched at something to stop it in its tracks. "You were holding that cat—" he looked at her accusingly "—just before you dished up my food!"

"I washed my hands in the laundry room. For heaven's sake, Jordan, sit down and try not to be so difficult. Since I'm going to be head cook and bottle washer from now on, you'd better get used to—"

"I didn't hire you as a cook!" He scowled at her. "You're here to look after Mandy. Period. Don't include *me* in your plans to play house!"

"I'm not here to *play* house." Exasperation threaded her voice. "This is for *real,* Jordan. I want to make Mandy happy, and for that, the child needs a warm, secure and loving home. I need to be the next best thing to a mommy to her. And that means doing 'mommy' things, like cooking and cleaning and—"

"I don't need a cook/housekeeper! I can cook for myself, and I hire an excellent cleaning company to—"

"But I don't *want* to be your—quote—cook/housekeeper. I know I can never be Mandy's *mother,* but I don't want her to think of me as a servant, either. I want her to experience the things mothers and daughters do together—like dusting, and tidying cupboards, and making cookies, and arranging flowers, and—''

"Point taken.'' His own voice sounded dour, churlish. "So," he said grudgingly after a few moments, "am I to understand you want me to cancel the cleaning company? You'll do *everything* yourself?''

"Yes." She sighed. "Look, I know you don't like me—and to be truthful, I don't know yet how I feel about you. So far," her tone was dry, "I have to admit I'm not favorably impressed. But for Mandy's sake, we must agree to live amicably. She's had enough stress in her young life without having to experience conflict between the two people who mean most to her—''

She paused as someone knocked on the outside door.

"Excuse me," she said. "That'll be Hugh." Crossing the kitchen, she unlocked the door and opened it.

On the stoop stood a very tall young man wearing a baseball cap, a striped sports shirt, and peacock blue Bermuda shorts. His grin was as wide as his shoulders.

"Hey, Fliss," he said. "You ready?''

"Come in," she said. "Meet my employer. I just have to pop upstairs and get my bag." She turned to Jordan. "This is Hugh Andrews, Jordan, an old friend. Hugh, this is Jordan Maxwell. I'll be right back…''

Jordan nodded curtly.

"Don't let me interrupt you," Hugh said, waving a hand towards the shepherd's pie. "Don't let your dinner get cold. Sit down, man.''

"It'll wait." Jordan shoved his hands into his pockets. "So…" he searched for something to say "…you've known Ms. Fairfax for some years?''

"I knew her brother first, actually. He was the one who introduced us.''

"Denny." The name grated on Jordan's ears. It seemed as if he was fated to meet people connected to—

"No, not Denny. He was older. It was the other brother, the younger one. Felicity's twin."

"She has a twin?" Good Lord, another Fairfax.

"Had." Hugh's face sobered. "Todd. He was a fisherman—died two years ago when his boat capsized in a storm."

As Jordan took this in, he heard steps approaching.

"Don't say anything about it," Hugh murmured quickly. "It devastated Fliss. She never talks about it."

When Felicity came into the kitchen, Jordan found himself looking at her in a new light. Looking at her *properly*, for the first time.

"I don't know when I'll be back," she said. "Could you give me a house key?"

All he'd seen previously, because he'd never wanted to let his eyes linger on her longer than absolutely necessary, was that she had a long blond braid, a generous mouth and wide-set gray eyes. Now, as he met those rather lovely gray eyes, he saw a hint of sadness there, which was in direct contradiction to her pleasant, questioning smile.

"Jordan?" She waved a hand before him. "Do you have a spare key?"

"Sure." He crossed to the desk under the wall phone and opening a drawer, fumbled around till he found the key he was looking for. He walked over to her. "There you are."

She held out a hand, and he saw a fretwork of faint lines on the palm. He also saw delicate blue veins at her wrist. How fragile she was. That surprised him, because although she was slim and slightly built, he had not thought of her as "fragile." She gave off such an aura of determination and self-confidence and energy.

He dropped the key onto her palm and she closed slender fingers around it. Her nails were neatly manicured, and buffed to a shine. Pretty hands. Feminine.

She smelled of wildflowers and citrus, romantic and energetic, a tantalizing and intriguing blend.

"When you've finished your shepherd's pie," she said, "you'll find some bread pudding in the oven."

With that, she followed Hugh outside, leaving him feeling confused and off balance, and unable to pin down the unsettling new emotions she'd stirred up inside him.

Felicity didn't get back to Deerhaven till almost two in the morning, but though sleepy and bone-tired, when Hugh dropped her off she had that satisfied feeling of a job well done.

"Thanks, Hugh, I owe you," she told him through his open window of his van. "I do appreciate all your help!"

"No problem." He looked up at the house. "Lights are all out."

Felicity yawned. "I'll have to be quiet."

"Have you got the bread and buns?"

"Right here."

"Don't forget to set your alarm!"

"It's going to be a short night!"

She watched him leave, and then went around to the back door.

Once inside, she put on the kitchen light, and after putting the bakeries away, noticed a note on the island. Expecting that Jordan might have written a few words to thank her for making dinner, she flicked it up and with a feeling of anticipation, she read what he'd written:

Don't forget to let that ★&%$★ cat out. He's been yowling like a banshee all night.

Ungrateful wretch! she muttered.

And screwing the paper into a hard little ball, she flung it, in a fit of pique, across the room.

Jordan cautiously opened the kitchen door just before seven next morning, half expecting to see the cat throwing up again. But there was no sign of him.

The only thing on the kitchen floor was a wad of paper.

He picked it up, unrolled it.

And saw the note he'd written the night before.

Remorse stabbed him. She must have been exhausted when she got back—he'd heard the car arrive, around two o'clock. She'd have come into the kitchen, feet dragging, glad to be home...only to be greeted by his bad-tempered complaint.

He put on his coffee, then wandered through to the front door and stepped out to the path to pick up his copy of the *Vancouver Sun* where the delivery man had tossed it.

Straightening, he inhaled a deep breath of the fresh summer-scented air. What a *great* day it was going to be. He took a moment to look around and savor the peace of the early morning. And the beauty of it. The sky was streaked with pink, the sun a blinding fiery ball in the east, the ocean an impossibly dazzling sheet of quicksilver.

"Isn't it a wonderful morning?"

He turned as Felicity's voice came from behind.

She stepped out to join him, and he couldn't help but notice how slim and attractive she looked in a dove-gray T-shirt and white capri pants. Despite her late night, her eyes were clear. And despite his surly note about her cat, her expression was friendly.

"Hi," he said. "You were out late."

"Oh, I'm sorry. I disturbed you. I did try to be quiet."

"I didn't hear you…just your friend's vehicle."

"Still…"

"No problem."

She slid her hands into the hip pockets of her pants. "What a terrific view you have," she said. "How long have you been in this house?"

"Ever since I got married. Ten years ago. I've been thinking of moving—but I can't. At least, not right now. I don't want to put Mandy through any unnecessary changes."

"That's a good idea. She really needs the security of the familiar surroundings."

As they walked back inside, she said, "Why would you want to move, though? Don't you like the house?"

"Do you?"

"I do like the layout. But…"

"Go on."

She gave a light shrug. "Well, when Mandy showed me over it yesterday, I have to admit I found it a bit stark—but that's just me," she added quickly, as they entered the kitchen. "I like a more homey look. Lived in. Loved in. This house doesn't have that—" She broke off and bit her lip. "I'm sorry. I didn't mean to imply—"

"But you're right." His tone was deliberately careless. "The house *is* stark. The furnishings *are* stark, and not to my taste, either. And although the place has certainly been *lived* in, it's a long time since—" Now it was his turn to break off. He had no intention of telling her that during the couple of years prior to Marla's death, relations between them had become strained and they had rarely had sex. And it had been a very long time before that that they'd actually made *love*. "Suffice it to say, the Waltons we were not."

"I'm sorry, Jordan, I wasn't criticizing. And I know you love Mandy." She toyed with the tail of her braid, which lay over one breast. "I'm well aware that her happiness is all-important to you—just as it is to me. I want her to learn to trust me again. It's going to take time to make her feel really secure with me, but I have all the time in the world. Can I ask you something?"

"Shoot."

"I was wondering…why do you have her sleeping in her crib again?"

"It was her idea, believe me. After it arrived here from your place, she insisted it be set up in her room, she refused to sleep anywhere else. Got quite hysterical, actually, when I tried to persuade her to sleep in her bed. So I didn't push it. I figured the crib was…is…a security thing for her. She won't even tolerate having the side left down when she's in it. I guess she feels cocooned and safe when it's up."

"I'll try getting her to sleep with it down, but not until she feels comfortable with it. And then maybe at some stage, when she's ready to leave her nest, she'll make the change to the bed herself. That would be the best way."

"I agree."

"Could I ask you one more question?"

"Sure." He took a mug from the cupboard. "Coffee?"

"No, thanks, I'll wait and have my breakfast with Mandy." As he poured his, she said, "I wanted to ask if I could use the empty room across from my bedroom, use it as a sewing room."

"No problem. You do a lot of sewing?"

"Quilting. I sell my work. And teach quilting at night school. Or have been. I taught the last class of the current session last week, so I'm free now." She smiled. "Thanks, I appreciate your letting me use the room." Glancing at her watch, she said, "I'll go upstairs now and check on Mandy. I just wanted to catch you before you left. Oh, one last thing…tonight for dinner I'm making chicken pie. Will you be home in time to eat with us and spend some time with Mandy? She didn't see you at all yesterday."

"I'll do my best."

"That's all I can ask." As she turned to go, she said, "Have a good day."

"You, too." And watching her leave, he almost called after her, "That was a fantastic meal you left for me last night." Almost. He opened his mouth to say the words, but though he knew he should pass her the well-deserved compliment, the bitterness in his heart, the bitterness he felt towards her brother Denny, wouldn't allow him to do so.

"Do you think," Felicity said to Mandy that afternoon after settling her down for her nap, "that we could leave the side of your crib down today?"

Mandy shook her head fiercely.

"OK." Felicity leaned over and dropped a kiss on the child's brow. "That's fine. Maybe another day."

"Where are you going, Fizzy?"

"To the kitchen to start making dinner. And when you get up we'll bake some cookies then take RJ for a walk."

Felicity hoped that Jordan would come home in time to eat with them, and then play with Mandy before she went down for the night. But failing that, she hoped he'd get home before she, herself, went to bed. She had asked him a couple of questions that morning, but she had kept one question, the *crucial* one, for later. She knew it would provoke a heated discussion, and maybe some angry words. But she couldn't carry on at Deerhaven till she got the answer she needed. It would be far too painful, in the long run, to both Mandy and herself if she didn't.

"Can I have a turn holding RJ's lead, Fizzy?"

"Yes...if you're careful." Felicity transferred the lead to Mandy's hand. "Hold tight."

"Nice kitty." RJ curled himself around one of Mandy's ankles, purring. "He remembers me, doesn't he!"

"Of course he does. After all, you've been friends since you were a baby!"

"I like him better than any of my stuffed toys." With a proud smile, Mandy led the cat across the front lawn. "Let's go for a walk, RJ."

Felicity stayed close to her, ready to grab the cat if he should tug himself free.

"I wanted a kitty of my own," Mandy said. "But you

know Mommy didn't like cats or dogs. She said they were messy and smelly, and a cat would wreck the drapes."

The child spoke matter-of-factly and didn't seem at all upset as she spoke of her mother. But it wasn't too surprising, for over the years that Felicity had baby-sat for Marla, she'd seen ample evidence that the woman had cared little for her daughter. Felicity had always found it unbearably sad—for both of them. How could anyone not love this dear sweet girl? It was beyond her understanding.

"Cats *can* make a mess, Mandy. They sometimes try to climb up the drapes, and they tear them…and sometimes they decide to sharpen their claws on the furniture. RJ used to when he first came to live with me but he doesn't anymore."

She cocked her ears as she heard the sound of a car coming up the drive. "I think your daddy's home." Taking the leash from Mandy, she said, "Let's go and see."

They entered the house through the sitting room's patio doors and by the time they reached the foyer, Jordan was coming in the front door. Felicity noticed that he looked very tired. But when he saw them, he dropped his briefcase and held his arms out to Mandy. "Hi, sweetheart!"

With a joyous "Daddy!" she ran to him and he swept her up and planted a kiss on her forehead.

"So," he said with a fond smile. "How was your day?"

She wrapped her arms around his neck and looked up at him adoringly. "It was a *good* day. How was yours?"

"It was a *busy* day!" He dropped her to the floor and glanced at Felicity. "Hi. Everything OK?"

"Yes, everything's fine. When do you want to eat?"

"Give me fifteen minutes to have a shower, unwind."

"Do you have to go out again?" she asked.

"No. Why?" He was already over at the stairs.

"I have something I need to discuss with you. I was hoping we could talk...after Mandy's in bed."

"Fizzy, can I feed RJ?" Mandy asked.

"Sure." Felicity handed her the loop of the leash. "Give him some of his dry food...not too much, just a few niblets."

As Mandy headed to the kitchen, bristling with self-importance, Jordan hovered, one hand on his newspaper. "What's it about?"

"I'd prefer to wait and—"

"Is there some problem?"

She hesitated. Then said, "Not unless you make it one."

"Can't you at least give me a clue?"

"It's to do with Mandy—"

"Yeah?"

"And...the future. Our future, Mandy's and mine."

His expression became guarded. "Ah." He tugged open his tie, undid the top button of his shirt. Easing his jaw up, as if he still felt the collar shackling him, he said, "Why don't we just take it one day at a time—"

"I'm afraid that's not good enough. Not for me. Not for Mandy. And in the long run, probably not for you, either. We have to talk. And I don't want to put it off."

He gave an irritable shrug. "In that case, OK. Not right after dinner, though. I want to spend time with Mandy. Then I have to do some work on my computer—

and before I can get on with that, I have to call technical support to get instructions about some complex software I've just installed. It may take a while.''

''Around nine o'clock then?''

''Later,'' he said firmly. ''Come to my study at ten. I should be all clear by then.''

He turned and walked up the stairs, determination in the set of his shoulders, the firmness of his steps.

Felicity watched him go, and felt a quiver of apprehension. Jordan Maxwell was going to be a mighty adversary in the battle of wills that lay ahead.

But it was a battle she simply had to win.

CHAPTER FOUR

JORDAN flicked an irritated glance at his watch. Ten-fifteen. Was the woman trying to make a point—the point being that she wasn't about to say "How high?" when he told her to jump?

Frustration rippled through him as he strode out of his study and bounded up the stairs.

Her bedroom door lay open, and the room was in darkness. But the door of her sewing room also lay open and its light was on.

Incensed by her show of defiance, he marched toward it. Whatever it was she wanted to talk to him about would have to wait till tomorrow. He'd tell her in no uncertain terms that—

He halted abruptly at the sewing room door and gaped in disbelievingy.

When had all this...*stuff* arrived: the comfy-looking green couch, the velvet wing chairs, the antique rosewood coffee table? Not to mention the Chinese rug, in pinks and greens, and the rosewood bookcase set in the alcove by the fireplace, its shelves crammed with books!

RJ was curled up in a corner of the couch, dozing. And Ms. Fairfax was curled up in one of the velvet wing chairs—dozing, too. A piece of quilting lay on her lap. At her elbow, on a side table, was a pot of tea and a mug. And from a sleek white ghetto blaster atop the rosewood bookcase drifted Mozart's Piano Concerto in D minor.

Ms. Fairfax had moved in.

Ms. Fairfax had *taken possession.*

Dumbfounded, he took a step forward.

A floorboard creaked under his foot.

Ms. Fairfax's eyes flew open, and when they lit on him, her expression became dismayed. "What time is it?"

"Quarter after ten."

Face flushing scarlet, she scrambled to her feet. "Oh, I'm *sorry.* I fell asleep. I guess my late night last night caught up with me and—" Her quilting slid to the carpet, and with a vexed murmur, she bent to pick it up.

Darn it, he had misjudged her. It was obvious she was sincere and had not set out to defy him. "No problem." He waved a hand around. "Where did all this come from?"

"I hope you don't mind. They're from my apartment. I'd originally planned on sending everything to the island, and my mom was going to store it in her basement till I found a place of my own. But when I called to tell her I was here, she suggested I keep my belongings here, too. And since you'd already told me I could use this room, I thought—"

"Sure, it's OK—"

"You don't mind?"

"Of course not."

"And it means I can have my own private sitting room, for when I have friends to visit."

He had never envisaged her having visitors.

"Now that *is* going to be a problem." He found himself scowling. "You can't entertain men up here, it wouldn't be a good example to set Mandy."

She stiffened. "You don't have to tell me what is or

is not a good example for Mandy. I have no intention of having men up here."

"Good. As long as that is clear." He didn't want her having men here...but didn't stop to figure out why—although he knew it didn't entirely have to do with Mandy.

"I've stored some boxes in your basement. In a corner. They won't be in your way."

"Fine."

She'd turned her attention to the piece of quilting in her hands, turning it carefully over, inspecting it. He heard a soft, "Tsk!"

"What's the matter?" he asked.

"I've lost my needle." She put the quilting down and searched the chair. Then she shook her head.

"No luck?" he asked.

"It must be on the floor." Crouching down, she peered around, and ran a hand charily over the carpet. "I'll have to find it. Someone might step on it...Mandy..."

He stood for a few moments, before deciding he could hardly walk away and leave her to it. Getting down on his haunches beside her, he joined the search.

After several seconds, she said, "Oh, thank goodness, there it is!" She picked it up from just beside his right foot, and leaning past him, set it on the coffee table. But as she made to get up, she lost her balance and toppled against him. She knocked him sideways and they fell together. He ended up flat on his back, she ended up sprawled inelegantly on top of him.

Her face was so close to his, he could see every single lustrous lash that fringed her startled eyes.

It was a long time since he'd had a woman on top of

him. And this one was feminine and feather-light, with honey-scented breath and a golden braid that had fallen over his neck like a heavy silk rope. Through her knit top he felt the firm swelling of her breasts; through his jeans, he felt the pressure of pelvic bones and thighs. The sensation was arousing.

His reaction was instantaneous.

Before she could catch her breath, he had grasped her shoulders, with every intention of lifting her off...but instead, driven suddenly by an instinctive primal urge, he pulled her down instead, and kissed her.

Silk soft lips. The scent of wildflowers and citrus. The taste of honey. Sweet, so sweet—

He wanted more. He took more. Deepening the kiss, he gave in to his rising desire—

She wrenched herself away from him. Clambering to her feet, she stumbled back and looked down on him with an expression of consternation. Her hands clenched and unclenched, her breasts rose and fell agitatedly.

He lay, defenceless and vulnerable, gathering himself together as best he could. Then cursing silently, he hoisted himself up and stood facing her.

"You don't have to say it." Anger—with himself—roughened his voice. "That was out of line." Her T-shirt had ridden up and he tried to ignore the slice of naked midriff. "And it was a huge mistake. You needn't worry. It won't happen again—"

"No," she said breathlessly, "It certainly won't!"

"Under the circumstances—"

A loud wail came from Mandy's room.

Looking as if she couldn't wait to get away, Felicity rounded him quickly, keeping as far from him as she could. "We'll have to postpone our talk till tomorrow," she said in a rush. "In the meantime—"

"In the meantime—" he called after her as she fled "—I'm going to forget this little incident ever took place, and I'd be greatly obliged if you would forget it, too."

More easily said than done.

Felicity spent a restless night, disturbed by dreams of Jordan.

And The Kiss.

When she woke, early, she sat up in bed, hugged her duvet around her knees, and stared abstractedly into space.

His lips had been warm, firm, sensual. The kiss itself…absolutely blissful.

Like no kiss she'd experienced before.

But then he was like no man she'd ever kissed before. And as his lips had moved so passionately on hers she'd felt him steal something from her—was it maybe a corner of her *heart?*—and for one wild moment she'd been tempted to surrender, to take whatever his kiss was promising, to let it take her wherever it might lead.

But common sense had prevailed. She'd torn herself free…and was grateful he'd never know how difficult that had been.

She got out of bed, and walked over to the dresser mirror. Her cheeks were flushed, her eyes too bright, and her lips…weren't they just a little puffy?

She looked, she realized with a pang of dismay, not only like a woman who had been passionately kissed, but a woman who was teetering on the brink of falling in love.

And wouldn't falling in love with this particular man be the most foolish thing she had ever done?

Jordan wasn't around much during the rest of the week and Felicity didn't get a chance to talk with him privately.

On Sunday, however, he came home in the early afternoon. It had been bucketing down with rain all day and she was in the basement, taking a yellow rain slicker from one of her boxes, when he came pounding down the wooden stairs.

"Oh, hi, this is where you are!" He shook out an enormous black umbrella and propped it, open, on the floor.

"I thought you had to show an open house?"

"It was canceled. The place sold this morning."

"So you're off for the rest of the day?"

"Yup. I came home to spend some time with Mandy."

"She's still sleeping." Felicity held the slicker to her chest. "Jordan, we need to talk—"

"About...?"

"I told you *days* ago that I need to talk to you about Mandy...and the future."

"Oh." He shoved his hands in his pants pockets, jangled his keys. "That's right. We didn't quite get around to it, did we!"

His tone had a tinge of irony. Felicity's cheeks grew warm as she remembered the circumstances that had led to the postponement of their talk. "Do you have time now?"

"Sure." He ambled over to the stairs and stood aside

for her to ascend first. "Were you thinking of making tea?"

"I wasn't, actually, but I'll make us a pot."

As they walked to the kitchen, he nodded toward her slicker. "You planning to go out?"

"If the rain eased off a bit, I was going to take Mandy for a walk. But since you want to spend time with her—"

"I do. You can take the rest of the afternoon off—have a break from baby-sitting, go visit friends."

She made no reply.

But as they sat at the table a few minutes later with a mug of tea before them, she said, "That's just what I mean."

"What's just what you mean?"

"Telling me to take the rest of the afternoon off." She regarded him with ill-concealed frustration. "You're treating me as if I'm a servant!"

He gave her a puzzled "Well, aren't you?" look.

"I told you," she said, "that I want to be like a mother to Mandy. How can I *feel* like a mother, if you treat me like a servant, one who can be given an afternoon off...or, equally, can be dismissed on a whim." She added, watching carefully for his reaction, "You and I *are* both in this for the long term, aren't we?"

He didn't even wriggle uncomfortably in his chair. Cool as could be, he said, "The best thing for us is to take everything one day at a time—I believe I already said that to you."

She lurched to her feet, cheeks aflame. "To *me* you did. But to *Mandy* you said something *completely* different!"

"What are you talking about?"

"You told your daughter that you'd be booting me out the moment you had someone to take my place." She planted a fist on her hip and glared down at him. "You're a snake, Jordan Maxwell! A deceitful, conniving—"

"Hey, hey, hey!" He pushed to his feet and glared back at her, his green eyes flashing with anger. "Just one minute! I've never said any such thing to Mandy or anyone else!"

"I *heard* you!"

She almost stepped back as his expression darkened. But she held her ground.

"I don't know," he snapped, "What Mandy's been saying to you but—"

"Not Mandy. *You* were the one who said it. That first day I was here, you came home around seven and went into Mandy's room—she was asleep but you spoke to her—"

"How do you know—"

"I was in the room, too, but you didn't see me," she said grimly. "I was dozing, on the bed, but your voice woke me up and I was just in time to hear you tell Mandy not to get too attached to her 'precious Fizzy' again, because you were going to ease her out as soon as you possibly could."

"Ah." He blew out a breath. "That." He had the grace to look chagrined. Shamefaced.

A sly fox, as well as a snake, Felicity thought scornfully. "Yes," she retorted.

"Ah."

"I can't stay here under these circumstances. But," she hastened to add, "it's my own fault. I was so desperate to see Mandy again, I didn't think the matter through when you came to me for help. I should have got some guarantee from you *then* that my position would be permanent. I can't think of anything worse for Mandy than having me here only to have me leave again. But better to leave right now, than three months down the road when she would, I hope, be trusting me again. Have you any idea how abandoned she must have felt after—''

''Of course I do. I took her to a top-notch therapist and I've followed the woman's advice—''

''What did she say?''

''She told me to keep Mandy close, give her lots of cuddling and comfort, spend as much time as I could with her, just be there for her. Help her feel secure—''

''And how secure will she feel if I 'abandon' her *again?*''

''I'd planned on having someone else here, for as long as it took to get Mandy to love her, before I let you go.'' Jordan suddenly looked so helpless she felt a stab of pity.

In a gentler voice, she said, ''I know you love Mandy, and I know that she loves you. But I truly believe she needs *both* of us in her life. She needs the continuity. At the same time, I know I'm the last person you want in your house. So it's entirely up to you, what happens now. But you have to be honest with me, Jordan. If you still plan to ease me out, I won't hang around. I'll leave today. Now.''

''You mean that, don't you!''

''Yes, I do.''

''You're tougher than you look, Felicity Fairfax!''

''When I have to be.'' She gazed at him steadily. ''So...what's your decision?''

"I don't have a choice, do I! Okay, you stay. And I won't try to ease you out."

"Do I have your word?"

"You want something in writing?"

"Your handshake will do."

He came around the table, and she held out her hand. He grasped it. His skin was warm, his clasp firm. "Ms. Fairfax," he said, "You've got yourself a deal."

For the rest of the week Felicity saw little of Jordan.

When he was at home, he spent as much of his time as possible with Mandy, and on those occasions, Felicity kept out of his way.

But on Saturday, he arrived home in time for dinner and they all ate together. Afterwards, he played ball in the garden with Mandy, and later he put her to bed. When he came downstairs, Felicity was in the sitting room, gathering up the toys Mandy had been playing with earlier.

"One step forward," he said as he came into the room. "Mandy asked me to leave the side of her crib down."

"She did?" Felicity beamed at him. "Oh, that's wonderful! I'm so pleased."

"Yeah, it's good."

Before dinner, he'd changed out of his business suit and was wearing a black tank top and black shorts. His jaw was shadowed, his hair disheveled…his charisma bone-melting! And his eyes, those seductive green eyes, were, for once, warm as they locked with hers.

She remembered The Kiss and felt a wave of panic. Don't look at me like that, she begged him silently. You're going to make me fall in love with you.

She could feel it happening. She wanted to be in his arms, wanted to lose herself in him—

"Are you OK?" His brisk voice startled her.

"Me? Oh...yes, I'm fine."

"You look a bit...dizzy."

"No, I'm fine. Just a bit...well, you know, just so happy that Mandy's making progress."

He wandered around the room. Crossed to the window. Stood with his back to it, facing her.

"Next Sunday," he said, "is the office picnic. We've always gone, as a family. I hadn't mentioned it to Mandy till now as I wasn't sure if she'd be up to it this year. I thought maybe she wouldn't be able to handle the crowds, but I asked her just now if she'd like to go, and she's really excited already. What do you think?"

"Sure, if she wants to go you should take her."

"You'll come, too."

"Oh, I don't think—"

"She won't go unless you come along. It's a family occasion...and didn't you make it more than clear that you wanted to be considered part of this family?"

"Yes, but only—"

"Only when it suits you?" He shook his head. "Uh-uh. It doesn't work that way."

"It's not that I want to pick and choose! It's...well, in this case, all your colleagues will be there, and their wives, and—"

"So?"

"It'll be...awkward. I'll feel out of place."

"You'll be with me."

Little did he know that that was the problem! The more she saw of him, the more she liked him. And spending time with him, in a family picnic atmosphere, was going to fill her with longings for things that could never be. And that was the real reason she was so reluctant to go.

But she wasn't about to tell him so.

"Then," she said lightly, "I'll look forward to it. Let's hope that we get a nice sunny day."

They did.

When Sunday rolled around, an early morning haze over the ocean soon burned off, and by the time they set off for Ambleside Beach, where the picnic was to be held, the day was sunny and clear and already very hot.

The drive from Deerhaven took ten minutes, and Mandy chattered all the way. Seated in the front, between her father and Felicity, she was so excited she could barely sit still.

"I have my swimsuit on," she burbled to her father. "My new yellow one, under my shorts and top. And I made Fizzy pack her bikini, too, so she can go in the races and some of the races are in the water, right, Daddy?"

"Right." He kept his eye on the road as they turned off Marine Drive, down Thirteenth Street, across the railway tracks and into the park. "Lucky it's such a nice day. Not like a couple of years ago, when we were rained out."

Felicity had no intention of wearing her bikini but she'd packed it just to keep the peace. When the time came for the races, she would come up with some excuse.

After they'd parked, Mandy hovered close while her father and Felicity unloaded the trunk, Jordan lifting out a couple of loungers while Felicity took charge of the capacious straw bag containing sunscreen, towels, and all their other paraphernalia.

Jordan slammed the trunk lid, and hefted up the loungers while Felicity took Mandy's hand in hers. Then all three walked across the lawn to the beach area.

"Where do they hold the picnic?" Felicity asked.

"Over by those tables." Jordan nodded towards a group of picnic tables set up on the grass on the north side of the Seawalk path that ran parallel to the beach. "Handy to the water. And lots of space for the kids to run around."

Felicity could see about fifty or sixty people over by the tables, a few of them seated, most of them standing talking to each other. She felt a bit nervous. Not that she didn't like people, she did, but it always took her a while to get over the initial shyness. And the way this lot were chattering, it looked as if they were old friends.

Jordan said, "There's Todd Ross, Mandy." He indicated a child running around with a kite, a little apart from the main group. "Why don't you go over and talk to him? Remember what fun you had with him last year?"

A bunch of children went screaming past, chasing after a red beach ball. All appeared to be having a super time.

"I don't want to talk to him just now." Mandy pressed close to Felicity. "I want to stay with Fizzy."

"Sure," her father said. "That's fine."

When they reached the group, he set up the loungers. Then turning to Felicity, he said, "C'mon, I want you to meet some people."

* * *

Felicity fit in beautifully and Jordan had to admit he'd never enjoyed the annual picnic so much.

Watching "Fizzy" now, as she built sandcastles with Mandy and Todd and three other preschoolers, he couldn't help comparing her with Marla.

Marla had accompanied him to the picnics but she'd never played with Mandy, in fact had spent no time at all with her. She'd always been dressed up in some stunning new eye-catching outfit, with her makeup impeccable, and she'd flirted all afternoon with his male colleagues.

He knew the wives talked about her.

Felicity on the other hand hadn't looked twice at any of the men. She'd been very polite and friendly when introduced around, but it was the women she chatted with after. And she'd been a hit.

Sitting alone at the top of the beach, sifting sand between his fingers, he allowed himself to look at her.

She was wearing a blue bikini and a battered old straw sun hat. Her hair was in its usual casual braid, her only makeup a dash of raspberry lipstick. She looked as if she was having the time of her life.

He hadn't known she was suffering from a headache till Mandy had asked her to change into her bikini. The child had come up to them while they were helping set the tables for the picnic.

"It's time for the water races," she said to both of them. "You have to change into your swimsuits now."

"OK, honey. Felicity, we can finish this later."

"I'll finish up," she said. "I'm going to skip the races. Sorry, darling," she'd said to Mandy, with a rueful smile. "I have a headache, and running around won't help it any."

"Do you want an aspirin or something?" he'd asked.

"No, I'll be fine. I should have put on my sun hat much earlier than I did, that's all."

"OK. C'mon, then, Mandy, let's—"

"I'm not going." Mandy's eyes had filled with tears. "I'm not going if Fizzy can't go. You know I wouldn't leave Fizzy when she's not feeling well."

Helplessly, he stood there, not knowing how to cope.

After an awkward silence, Felicity said, "My headache's not really that bad, sweetie. Maybe if I don't run too fast, it'll be OK."

Mandy wiped a forearm over her eyes. "Really?"

Felicity gave her a hug. "Yes, really. Let's get my bikini and find the changing rooms." Throwing Jordan a glance over her shoulder, she said, "Back in a tick."

Something in her expression had led him to believe that she hadn't had any headache; she just hadn't wanted to appear in a bikini.

And now, as he looked at her, he wondered why on earth not. She had a fabulous figure, lithe and curvy and—

"So, Jordy, you got yourself a live one!"

Jordan turned as Jack LaRoque crouched down beside him.

"Hey, Jack. Live one? What do you mean?"

"I'm talking about your...house guest. You lucky dog. Where did you find her, man...the fabulous Felicity?"

Jordan wanted to punch him. Didn't want to hear Felicity's name on his lecherous lips. "Ms. Fairfax is an employee. She's been Mandy's caregiver for years."

"You mean you and the babe aren't...involved?"

"That's right."

"Then," Jack sprang up, and stretched, "you'll have no objection to my making a move on her?"

Before Jordan could answer, the office Lothario took off down the beach towards the unsuspecting Felicity.

CHAPTER FIVE

JORDAN glared after him.

Jack LaRoque boasted that he could always get a woman into bed by the third date. And after he'd slept with his conquests, he moved on.

"Every gorgeous babe is a challenge," he'd been heard to say. "But hey, buddy, who wants to climb the same mountain twice...the view's gonna be just the same!"

Now he was crouching down beside Felicity, and she'd turned her head to look at him. Her expression was questioning. He said something. She laughed. Even from here, Jordan could hear the tinkling sound. He said something else, and she stood up. Moved a little way from the children. He followed her.

They stood talking. He had his hands casually on his slim hips, she brushed sand from her bare arms...but her eyes were upraised to his, her raspberry-lipsticked mouth set in a thoughtful pout.

Jordan reluctantly admitted they made a very attractive couple, she in her bikini, he in a pair of aquamarine trunks that set off his sun-bronzed body and his ash-blond hair.

But as LaRoque touched Felicity's arm and she didn't back away, Jordan felt a twinge of concern. By bringing her to the company picnic, he had unwittingly tossed her to this wolf. Shouldn't he do something to protect her?

What was the guy saying anyway? Was he asking her

out? Whatever it was, she was amenable to it. She was leaning toward him, smiling at him, her body language saying it all.

Dammit, Jordan thought, I've got to put a stop to this.

He surged to his feet and started toward them...but he was too late. LaRoque had already turned from her and was loping off along the beach.

Jordan hesitated, and was going to turn back, but Felicity had spotted him. She stood there, waiting for him.

He would look foolish now if he did an about-turn, so he continued on toward her.

"Hi," she said as he drew near. "What's up?"

"Nothing." He noticed that her cheeks were flushed and her eyes had an odd sparkle. "You were talking with LaRoque. What did he have to say for himself?"

Her flush deepened. "Oh, this and that."

He had asked her out and she'd accepted. Why didn't she want to tell him? And why couldn't he let it go?

"How did you like him?" he asked.

"Why?"

"Just wondered."

"I don't know him, so I can't—"

"Hey, Jordie!"

Jordan turned as someone called to him from behind. Todd's father waved to him from the top of the beach. "Bring the kids up, food's ready!"

Felicity seemed glad of the opportunity to curtail her conversation with Jordan.

"Gather up your spades and pails," she said to the children as she leaned over to help. "It's time to eat."

Jordan dragged his gaze from her cute little behind. Sure, she was attractive, but he mustn't let himself get involved with her private affairs. If she wanted to go out with Jack LaRoque, that was her own business. And if she got hurt, that was her own business, too.

He himself had made a huge mistake when he'd kissed her.

And he'd almost made another mistake, there, by trying to protect her from LaRoque.

If Felicity Fairfax was anything like her brother—and it was surely in her genes—she didn't need his protection. In all likelihood, Jack LaRoque was the one who would need protection from her.

"Is your head all better now, Fizzy?"

Felicity paused over the last crumbs of her hamburger and looked across the picnic table at Mandy. "Yes, it's all better."

She, Mandy and Jordan were at the same table as Todd and his parents, and another couple, Rhoda and Brett, who had a three-month-old baby girl, Selena.

"You were fortunate," Jordan drawled, "that it was so mild and passed so quickly...and you were able to put on your bikini and join in the races."

He was sitting across from her and she could see, by his mocking expression, that he'd guessed she'd had no headache. But surely he couldn't have figured out that he was the reason she hadn't wanted to put on the bikini?

Before she could respond, Mandy said, "She looks a knockout in her bikini. That's what Mr. LaRoque told her." The child popped the last corner of her hot dog into her mouth and looked at him innocently. "That's what he said, an absolute knockout."

Felicity stifled a groan and lowered her gaze to her empty plate. She'd had no idea that Mandy had overheard any of her conversation with Jack LaRoque. What else had she heard? What else was she going to say? Thank heaven the other two couples were engaged in a lively discussion about hockey.

"He said that, did he?" Jordan drawled.

"Yup. And then he said he'd love to take her dancing."

"He did, did he?" Jordan's tone was amused, but under the amusement Felicity sensed a hard edge.

She decided it was time to redirect the conversation. But before she could, Mandy piped up,

"And *then* Fizzy said—" The child broke off with a gasp. "Look, Todd, that crow took Lois Cooke's hot dog!" She swiveled around on the bench to follow the flight of the crow. It glided down and lit about thirty feet away.

Todd cried, "C'mon, Mandy, let's chase it!"

"Can we, Daddy?" Mandy asked.

"Sure, off you go."

The two excused themselves and then ran helter-skelter towards the crow, shrieking as they went.

In order to escape Jordan's assessing gaze, Felicity slid across the bench to look at Rhoda's baby, who was in her mother's arms, and sucking from a bottle of milk.

"She's lovely, Rhoda. So sweet."

"She's a chosen child," Rhoda said. "I can't have children," she went on matter-of-factly, "So Brett and I decided to adopt. We had Selena when she was just ten days old. We're very lucky." She gazed dotingly down on the child. "Blessed, really."

"Oh, you are." Felicity caressed the baby's dark curls. "She's just darling. May I hold her?"

"Sure. Just let me take that bottle, she's had enough."

Rhoda transferred her daughter to Felicity who cuddled the infant in her arms and looked down at her in the same doting way Rhoda had. "She's dozing off. Look at those gorgeous dark eyelashes! Oh, she's so pretty..."

"I can see you love babies," Brett said. "You planning on having any of your own?" he teased.

"Not at the moment," she said with a light laugh. "I've got my hands full looking after Mandy."

"How long have you been caring for her?" Rhoda asked.

"Since she was a baby."

"Then you must love her as if she were your own!" Rhoda said. "They don't take long to steal their way into your heart. With Selena...for Brett and me, it was love at first sight. And I remember Jordan being the same with Mandy, right, Jordan?"

"Yeah, love at first sight." He glanced around the group as he spoke, a smile in his eyes, but when his gaze met Felicity's, his smile faded. She saw a flicker of...something. And felt as if they'd suddenly become enclosed in a bubble of awareness. Nobody else existed. It was exciting, electrical, breathtaking. And then...

Mandy hurtled back and the moment was shattered.

"Fizzy!" She danced up and down. "I need to go to the bathroom."

Felicity surrendered the baby to Rhoda, and excusing herself from the table, took Mandy to the ladies' washrooms.

By the time they came back, cake and ice cream had been served, the conversation at their table had become general, and to Felicity's relief Jordan's glance at her was casual.

About an hour later, the couples with babies and small children began to drift away. And shortly after, Jordan suggested it was time they should be getting home, too.

So amid a flurry of goodbyes, they gathered up their belongings and made for the car. Within a few minutes they were driving out of the park, and up to Marine Drive.

Jordan glanced at his daughter. "Did you have a good time, Mandy?"

"Yes, Daddy." She yawned, and leaned sleepily against Felicity's shoulder. "Did you?"

"Sure did. How about you, Felicity?" He looked at her briefly over top of Mandy's head. "You seemed," he added dryly, "to be a hit with all and sundry."

She refused to take the bait. "I had a great time, thanks." She glanced down at Mandy, saw her eyes had closed. "I met some really interesting people."

"Yeah, I bet."

Ignoring his dry tone, she said, "Rhoda and Brett are lucky, having such a lovely little baby. So many people can't have children, and have to wait so long to adopt."

"Yeah. They're very happy. But—" he lifted one shoulder in a shrug "—it wouldn't be for me."

"What?"

"Taking on somebody else's kid. It could never be the same. For example, you'd never convince me that your feelings for Mandy could come anywhere near as deep as mine. It's a matter of blood, and genes, and family."

"I believe you're wrong, Jordan." Felicity stroked Mandy's silky curls, and noticed they were sprinkled with sand. "But it's not something we can ever measure, can we?"

He slowed as they reached the intersection of Marine Drive and Twenty-first Street, and then after turning right on the green light, he drove up the hill. "Someday," he murmured, "you may have a baby of your own. *Then* come and tell me you don't love her more than you love my daughter."

Jordan felt restless that evening and knowing he wouldn't sleep, he stayed up late. Hoping a drink would help him relax, he poured himself a whiskey and ensconced himself in an armchair in the living room.

It had been an odd day.

He hadn't wanted to spend it with Felicity, but once at the picnic, he'd not only enjoyed being there, he'd enjoyed her company. He'd enjoyed looking at her and watching her play with Mandy. The only part he hadn't enjoyed was watching her with Jack LaRoque.

Should he warn her about him?

Or would she read something into that?

Would she think he was…jealous?

Was he?

The thought dismayed him.

Certainly she was very attractive, with her heavy blond braid, her lovely gray eyes, her curvy figure. But it was more than just her looks that appealed to him. It was the graceful way she moved, and her sunny personality, and—

Who was he kidding? She was sexy as hell, an absolute knockout.

Jack LaRoque had been spot-on.

Felicity Fairfax could have most any guy she wanted. So why, he wondered, had she never married? Why—

The door behind him creaked.

He turned his head.

The object of his musings was standing in the doorway, an apologetic expression on her glowing, scrubbed face. Wearing a candy-striped shortie robe and with her hair in its usual single braid, she looked like a teenager on her way to a slumber party.

"I'm sorry," she said. "No...please don't get up. I won't stay. It's just...I couldn't sleep, so I came down to make some hot chocolate, and I saw the light on in here, thought you'd gone to bed and forgotten to switch it off."

He got up anyway, and turning for a moment, set his glass on the mantelpiece before swiveling around again. "Before you go...can I ask you something?"

"What?"

"How old are you?"

She raised her eyebrows. "I'm twenty-seven."

"You're kidding! You look a lot younger."

"I know." A smile lifted one corner of her mouth. "I still get asked for ID when I buy wine at the liquor store."

"That doesn't surprise me."

"Why do you want to know?"

"It's really none of my business, but when you go out on your date with Jack LaRoque—" He grimaced. "Nah, forget it. As I said, it's none of my business."

"But it is your business, Jordan." Her eyes had taken on a flinty hardness. "Do I have to hit you over the head with a two-by-four before you get the message? I'm not 'the baby-sitter,' I don't have nights off where I go dancing with any Tom, Dick or Jack. When are you going to start seeing me as a...part of your family?"

"You can't spend every moment of your time with

Mandy and me," he growled. "Don't you want to meet somebody, get married? Have children of your own?" Frustration had raised his voice. "I saw the way you looked at that baby today. Good grief, Felicity, get a life!"

Her face grew very pale.

"I do have a life, Jordan. Here. You just don't get it, do you! My life is Mandy. I couldn't love her more if she were my own—though I know I'll never convince you of that. And as for Jack LaRoque, give me credit for some sense. I've met his type before. If you really thought I'd go out with him...well, it shows how little you know me. And don't you think that should worry you, since you've put your daughter in my care?"

"Hey, don't get so het up! I was just looking out for you."

"I can look out for myself. I've been doing it for a long time." She tilted her chin. "Now if that's all—"

"And as for putting Mandy in your care, you didn't give me any choice. It was either your way or the highway!"

"Let's not get into that again!"

"No." He scraped a weary hand through his hair and turned away from her to pick up his glass from the mantelpiece. "Let's not. Go make your hot chocolate and get off to bed." Whiskey glass in hand, he turned around again to bid her goodnight.

But she had already gone.

For Felicity, the following days passed quickly.

She had settled in at Deerhaven and had come to feel at home there. As had RJ, who had claimed the Deerhaven grounds as his territory after having scrapped it out with a neighboring tom who had challenged him for possession.

Jordan drove himself hard at work, as if trying to make up for the months he'd taken off to spend time with Mandy. His hours were erratic, and it wasn't unusual for him to get home around midnight.

As a result, Mandy came to depend more and more on "Fizzy," and though she wasn't as clingy as she'd been in the beginning, she still didn't like to let her out of her sight.

And she still slept in her crib.

Felicity had continued, every once in a while, to try to coax her into using the bed again. Mandy just shook her head, and said, "No, Fizzy. I don't want to." And Felicity didn't pressure her. It did concern her, though, because although small for her age, Mandy would soon be feeling cramped in the crib.

But on the whole, the child seemed happy. And when Lacey visited, Mandy no longer hid behind Felicity as she had done at first, but greeted her with a shy smile.

"You've done a great job with my niece," Lacey said to Felicity when she popped around one evening. Jordan was out, and Mandy asleep. Lacey had brought a bottle of Chardonnay, and insisting Felicity have some, too, she had poured two glasses. Then she'd ushered Felicity out to the deck off the dining room, where they'd sat in cushioned loungers and watched the setting sun paint the western sky a magnificent red and the city smog a smouldering orange. "It's a long time," Lacey murmured, "since I've seen Mandy this relaxed and content."

"She still won't sleep in her bed." Felicity took a sip of her wine. "It worries me."

"All in good time." Lacey stretched out her long slender legs and kicked off her sandals. Running a careless hand through her mink-dark hair, she said, "Rome wasn't built in a day, Felicity. Now tell me, how are you and my brother getting along? Is he still as...difficult... as he was when you moved in first?"

"No, he's not difficult." What he was, was impossible! No, he wasn't impossible; the *situation* was impossible. She had become more and more attracted to him by the day, while ever since they'd exchanged words over Jack LaRoque, he had grown more and more distant. "He's always polite, always very gentlemanly."

"Oh, dear. He *is* being difficult!" Lacey pouted. "I know him when he's like that. He shuts himself off completely. You might as well batter your head against an oak tree as expect to get some emotion from him once he withdraws into himself. Not that he was ever very good at expressing his feelings but..." She rolled her eyes. "Aren't most men like that! Take Alice's husband, for example—"

"Alice?"

"Our sister—mine and Jordan's. Hasn't he mentioned her? Anyway, she's been married for ten years to this gorgeous-looking man who worships the ground she walks on but would you know it if you saw them together? Absolutely not. Dermid Andrew McTaggart would rather plant his bare size twelves in a blazing fire than show affection in public."

"I gather he's Scottish!"

"Aye." Lacey chuckled. "And a man of few words."

"Where do he and Alice live?"

"They have an alpaca ranch on Vancouver Island, not too far from Nanaimo."

"Do you see them often?"

"Actually, no. I love my sister dearly, but...I don't think the brawny Scot approves of me." She lifted one elegant shoulder in a shrug. "He doesn't think much of a woman—a *gurrl* as he calls me!—who makes her living by being photographed in exorbitantly expensive clothes. Alice makes all her own clothes—not only that, she's a fabulous cook, splendid housekeeper, helps out on the ranch—"

"Then it's no wonder he thinks the world of her," Felicity said. "She sounds like a perfect wife."

"She is...and now, to crown everything, she's pregnant. At last! They're thrilled to bits and it's been a long—"

The screen door opened and Jordan came out onto the deck. "Hi," he said. "When did you get home, Lacey?"

His sister stood up and greeted him with a kiss. "Early this morning. But I'm off again tomorrow to the Caymans."

"Everything all right today?" he asked Felicity.

Why did she always stiffen up inside when he was around? She'd been feeling so relaxed with Lacey. Now before she spoke, she had to concentrate to make sure her voice came out in a neutral tone, and steadily.

"Mandy's been fine," she said. "She did try to stay awake till you came home, but was too sleepy."

"I just couldn't make it. Sorry." He returned his attention to his sister. "Can you stay, Lace, have a sprig of parsley? Or maybe a lettuce leaf? A carrot stick?"

"Oh, stop teasing!" But Lacey's eyes twinkled. "We're not all as lucky as you, able to eat like there's no tomorrow and never gain an ounce! Although—" she ran an assessing gaze over him "—I think you've put on a bit of weight lately."

"It's all these dinners Felicity pushes on me." He grinned. "What's a guy to do? Can't waste good food."

"That's probably as close to a compliment as you're going to get from *this* man, Felicity." Lacey picked up her roomy leather bag which she'd slung over the back of the lounger. "He and Dermid McTaggart are a pair!"

She gave Felicity a quick hug. "I'm off now. Don't bother to see me out, I know the way."

And she was gone, pulling the screen door shut behind her, her sandals clicking neatly on the dining room floor as she left.

Jordan yawned. "Lord, I'm bushed." He collapsed onto the lounger his sister had vacated, and stretching out his legs, clasped his hands behind his head and lolled back. "What a day."

"Good...or bad?"

"I sold a two-million-dollar property just below the highway, it's been on the market for a year, finally got a buyer—but he voiced so many complaints about the house and the garden, and in such an arrogant way, that the vendor took umbrage and said no way was that man going to get his home. Fortunately I got him to see reason, but it was a close call."

"Have you eaten?"

He closed his eyes. "Haven't had time." He yawned again.

"I'll bring you out some curried chicken. And would you like a glass of beer?"

He squinted up at her. "Are you kidding?"

She smiled. "I'll be right back."

*   *   *

Sometimes he almost forgot she was who she was.

Like just now, when she'd looked down at him, her gray eyes alight with amusement. In that moment, she hadn't been Denny Fairfax's sister, she had just been an incredibly attractive young woman who wanted to make his life easier…and his only thought had been: *Jordan Maxwell, you are one lucky son of a gun!*

He blotted that thought out before it had time to take root. But he couldn't blot out the image of her enchanting smile, her laughing gray eyes.

Frustration shattered his lethargy, and he swung himself up and off the lounger. Felicity Fairfax threatened to sneak her way into his heart and he was having none of it. Bad enough that Mandy adored her and Lacey thought her wonderful. He certainly wasn't about to become involved any more than he had to with any member of the Fairfax family.

He'd maintained his distance from her ever since the day of the picnic. He'd slipped tonight, but only because he was so darned tired.

Crossing the deck, he leaned on the top of the railing and looked out over the ocean. The problem was, his heart had been empty for so long, it was vulnerable to—

The screen door opened.

He sent a last look out over the ocean, its darkening waters dotted with twinkling lights from anchored freighters, before turning.

Holding a tray in both hands, Felicity was trying to elbow the screen door shut.

Striding over to her, he took the tray. "Let me," he said. "Oh, this looks great. Thanks."

"You're welcome."

He carried the tray to the umbrella table, and as he set it down, he heard her close the screen door.

"I'll sit with you till I finish my wine," she said, and only then did he notice the two glasses on one of the small tables. One was empty, the other scarcely touched. She picked up the latter, and moved across the deck to sit on the swing seat. "I have something I want to discuss with you."

"OK." He dragged an upright lawn chair over to the table and sat down. Lifting his glass, he took a long swallow of his beer. Then he pulled the plate of curried chicken toward him. "What is it?"

She leaned back, and the setting sun painted her cheeks a rosy pink. "Mandy's outgrowing her clothes. We need to go on a shopping trip."

"No problem. I'll give you my credit card."

"Mandy wants you to come with us."

"Not possible." He buttered the warm roll on his side plate. "I'm far too busy."

"Jordan, she's hardly seen you lately."

He detected no criticism in her tone. Just concern. He sighed. "It's really not a good time."

"I know. But she *misses* you. It would mean so much to her. And is there ever really a good time?"

She was right. "Did you have any particular day in mind?"

"Whichever day would suit you...but soon?"

"Later on this week. OK? I'll take an afternoon off."

"Thank you." She got up, and wandered over to the railing. She stood with her back to him, looking out over the ocean, the way he had been doing a few minutes before.

He dug into the curry, and enjoyed every delicious

spicy morsel. The dessert was lemon mousse, light as a summer breeze. And the coffee, as usual, was excellent.

He tidied the tray, pushed it back. "That was terrific."

She turned. "I have something else to ask you. It's business." Her mouth lifted at one corner and her eyes had that amused sparkle again. "And I didn't want to discuss it with you while you were eating. It's about…my salary."

He set his elbows on the arms of his chair. Ah. She wanted more money. She knew she was indispensable. And now, he thought cynically, she was going to screw him for all she could get.

"Go on," he said.

"You're paying me the same salary I was getting when I baby-sat Mandy at the apartment."

To his surprise, he felt a sense of disappointment. It wasn't that she didn't deserve more money, she certainly did, and it was an oversight on his part that he hadn't taken up the matter sooner. It was just that "Fizzy" had begun to seem like part of the family, and he'd had the impression that money was of no importance to her. He'd thought nothing mattered to her but that she could be with Mandy. Ah, well, she was only human.

"Things are different now," she said. "I'm living in this lovely house, and I eat with the family. Jordan, you're paying me far too much—"

"Too *much?*"

"Yes. I'd like you to cut back my present salary to something more realistic."

"You're crazy! If anything, you deserve *more.* Without you, there would *be* no 'family' as such. Just me, in despair, and Mandy, miserable."

"I won't take more!" She sounded scandalized.

"And I won't give you less!" he retorted.

Suddenly, she laughed. "An impasse then."

Despite himself, he laughed, too. "Or a deal."

"So everything stays the same."

"It seems the only way."

He'd been wrong about her. Again. Was he never going to get a handle on how her mind worked?

Before he could figure anything out, the phone rang, out in the foyer.

He got up. "I'll get it."

He strode out and caught it on the fourth ring.

"Jordan Maxwell," he said.

"Is Felicity there, Mr. Maxwell? This is her mother."

He heard Felicity behind him and when he turned, he saw her crossing toward the kitchen, the tray in her hands.

"It's for you. It's your mother."

She set the tray down on the hall table, and with an anxious look on her face, hurried over.

She took the phone. "Hello—"

He picked up the tray and had started along the corridor to the kitchen when he heard Felicity say, with an anguished catch in her voice, "Oh, Mom, I'm sorry. Yes, of course I will…"

He hesitated. She sounded so upset. Then frowning, he continued on his way. He didn't want to become involved with any aspect of the Fairfax family's personal life.

In the kitchen, he disposed of his dishes and had just wiped the tray and set it on the counter when he heard Felicity come in.

He turned. Her face had a sickly cast and her dark-lashed gray eyes glistened with tears.

"Bad news?" he asked.

She nodded. "It's Denny. He...died a short time ago."

Jordan knew he should offer his condolences, say he was sorry. But it would ring false. So he said nothing.

"I have to go home on Thursday." Shivering, she wrapped her arms around herself. "For the funeral."

CHAPTER SIX

FELICITY phoned Joanne next morning to ask if she would drive her to Horseshoe Bay on Thursday morning, to catch a ferry to the island.

"Of course," Joanne said. "I'm so sorry about Denny, Fliss, but…you knew that with his injuries he was never going to get better, he's just been hanging on."

"I know. But still, it's hard."

"Of course it is. Look, I have to go now, but I'll see you on Thursday."

Felicity had left Mandy playing in the den when she went to make the call from the kitchen phone, but now, as she hung up the phone, the child piped up from the doorway, "Where are we going on the ferry, Fizzy?"

Felicity sat down at the table and held out her arms. "Come here, sweetie."

Mandy trotted over and Felicity took the child's hands in hers. "I have to go to Vancouver Island on Thursday but I'll be back that night. Your daddy's going to stay home from work and he's going to take you shopping for some lovely new outfits."

"No." Mandy's gaze was clear as she looked up at Felicity. "I'd rather come with you. I can go shopping any old time."

"I'm sorry, sweetie, you can't come with me."

"Why?"

Felicity knew Mandy had gone to her mother's funeral

and she didn't want to remind the child of what must have been a disturbing day. Reluctantly, she said, "I have to go to my brother's funeral."

"I can go to a funeral. I know how to behave."

"I'm sure you do, but people don't go to a funeral unless they know the person who died."

"Then I can sit outside the church and wait. I'm a good waiter. I can sit all day and wait if I have to."

"Sweetie—" Felicity made to pick Mandy up, meaning to take her on her knee, but the child wrenched back.

"You don't *want* me to come!"

"It's not that." Felicity got to her feet. "It's just—"

"And you won't come back. You'll never come back! I'll never see you again, just like before!"

Bursting into sobs, the child tore from the room, and as she took off along the corridor, Felicity hurried after her.

"Wait, Mandy—"

"Leave me alone!" Mandy had reached the stairs and scrambling up to the landing, she yelled, "Just go to your old funeral! I hate you and I don't *care* if you never come back! I don't ever want to see you again!"

Jordan came home in the late afternoon.

Felicity had been baking and had just taken some herb bread from the oven when he opened the back door.

Flushed from the oven's heat, she brushed her hands over her apron as she turned to greet him.

"Hi," he said. "Something smells good." He swung off his jacket and draped it over the back of the nearest chair. "So…" He looked around. "Where's Mandy?"

"I'm afraid there's been a bit of an upset, Jordan. I called Joanne to ask her to drive me to the ferry on

Thursday, and Mandy overheard me. She thought I'd be taking her with me, and when I said she couldn't come, she got quite hysterical. She ran up to her crib…and she's been there ever since. I can't make her budge. She hasn't eaten a thing since breakfast time.''

In a frustrated movement, Jordan ripped his tie off and undid the top button of his shirt. Tossing the tie on top of his jacket, he said, ''I'll talk to her.''

''Jordan, I'm really sorry. What can I do? I *have* to go to the funeral, but this is so distressing for Mandy—''

''Your brother, it seems, is still causing problems, even though he's no longer of this world!''

His harsh words scattered Felicity's feelings of guilt. ''That's a *horrible* thing to say! I can't believe you would say such a thing!''

''Believe it!'' he snapped, as he marched past her and out into the corridor. ''As far as this family is concerned, Denny Fairfax has produced nothing but trouble.''

After a quarter of an hour, when Jordan hadn't returned, Felicity decided to go looking for him. Not only did she want to know how he'd fared with Mandy, she wanted to tell him—and his daughter—that dinner was ready.

But when she reached the foot of the stairs, she heard Mandy sobbing up in her room, and the sound of Jordan's voice as he tried to quiet her down. Felicity desperately wanted to go up and see if she could help, but she held back. She'd had all day to break through but with no success. She had to give Jordan time.

Desolately, she went back to the kitchen. Checking that she hadn't forgotten anything on the table, and looking into the oven to make sure the dinner wasn't being burned, she sank down onto a chair, and setting her elbows on the arms of the chair, clasped her hands on her lap, and waited.

"Mandy's asleep."

Lost in thought, Felicity hadn't heard Jordan come into the kitchen. Now as the memory of his scathing comment returned to her, her expression became stony. Instead of being friendly and forthcoming as she usually was, she turned her hard gaze on him.

"Did you make any headway?" she asked.

"Yeah. It's all settled."

"She's happy to stay home with you?"

"No, she's going to the island."

"But she can't! I won't be able to look after her when I'm at the fun—"

"We'll all go."

Felicity blinked. "You mean…you'll come with us?"

He ran a hand over his nape. And looked at her wearily. "She won't go without me. She's afraid—"

"Afraid you'll be gone when she gets back. Oh, Jordan." Felicity's resentment quickly dissipated, to be replaced by compassion for Mandy. "Poor baby, she must be so confused and insecure, so…frightened."

"Yeah, she's frightened. So, here's the plan. We'll catch the ferry then I'll drive you to your mother's place. Mandy and I'll take off then and find something to do in town, till you're ready to leave."

"It's not really a town, more of a village. But there's a lake close by, with a really nice beach, and—" She broke off. "But are you *sure,* Jordan? It's an awful imposition."

"There's no alternative. At least, I don't see one. Do you?"

"No." She spoke softly. "I don't. Thank you. You've made the situation a whole lot easier, you've taken a load off my mind." She got up. "Are you ready to eat?"

"I don't have time now. I have to meet a client out in Eagle Ridge and I just dropped by to say hi—I did intend to have a bite to eat, but I didn't count on having to spend so much time with Mandy. Will it keep?"

"Yes."

"Good." He fastened his shirt button, put on his tie, then his jacket. He was halfway out the door before he called back, "Oh, by the way...about what I said earlier...I shouldn't have."

And with that he was gone.

It was as close to an apology as she would get, Felicity knew but she was content to accept it anyway.

The weatherman had forecast heavy rain for Thursday and his forecast proved correct.

A perfect day for a funeral, Jordan reflected, as he herded Felicity and Mandy from the ferry's car deck up the steep narrow stairs leading to the passenger deck. And both his companions seemed as somber as the weather. Felicity, a black raincoat over her black dress, had hardly spoken two words since they left Deerhaven. And Mandy, though brightly attired in a yellow top and shorts, with a purple slicker, was equally subdued.

The child had eaten only half a slice of toast for breakfast. And when he'd tried to coax her to eat more, she'd run crying from the kitchen.

Before going after her, Felicity had said, "She's still getting over her upset of the other day, Jordan. It was a backwards step. She's going to need lots of reassurance that neither one of us is ever going to desert her. It's going to take time. And patience. Do try not to worry.''

But how could he not? Mandy was his daughter. His own flesh and blood. And she meant more to him than anything else in the world.

Felicity held Mandy's hand firmly as Jordan ushered them to seats on the starboard side of the vessel.

After he'd helped them take off their coats, he ensconced them opposite each other in window seats, before tossing his leather jacket onto the bench beside Mandy.

''I'm going to get a coffee,'' he said. ''What would you like, Felicity?''

''I'll have a coffee, too,'' she said. ''Decaf. Thanks.''

''Mandy?''

''I'm not hungry.''

''I'll get you something, maybe you'll be hungry later. Keep my seat, sweetie,'' he added as a group of women approached.

Felicity watched him walk toward the cafeteria. And as he took his place in the already long lineup, she couldn't help noticing how he stood out in the crowd— not only because of his height and his dark good looks, but because he had such an air about him.

With a sigh, she gazed at him, loving his rugged profile, his lean figure, his—

''You're looking at Daddy.''

Felicity flicked her gaze to Mandy. ''Yes,'' she said. ''How did you know?''

'''Cos your eyes are soft.''

Jolted, Felicity realized she'd have to be more careful. Heavens, she'd have to be *much* more careful! ''He's a nice man," she said, and with a smile added, "Your own eyes are soft when you look at him."

"That's 'cos I love him." Mandy looked out the window. Her breath misted the pane, and with her fingertips, she wiped it clear. "I guess you love him, too."

Oh, Lord, what should she say to that? Deny it, and perhaps upset the child? Admit it…and have Mandy perhaps repeat it to her father?

It would be best, she decided, to give no response at all.

And it seemed Mandy didn't expect one. Her attention had flitted to a seagull gliding past the ferry.

Felicity ached to look at Jordan again. Instead, she took out the paperback mystery she'd brought with her.

And by the time he returned she was knee-deep in blood and dead bodies while an insane serial killer was just inches from attacking his next victim.

"Your coffee, madam!"

His voice startled her. She looked up, into a pair of amused green eyes.

"What's so funny?" she asked, taking the steaming mug from his outstretched hand.

"You." He nodded towards her book, *A Slice of Death,* and its macabre cover: a scalpel dripping with blood. "I hadn't figured you for the gory type."

Shoving aside his jacket, he sat down. "Here, Mandy, do you want these now?"

She looked without interest at the cardboard tray with its chocolate-chip muffin and a banana.

"No, thanks."

Jordan set the tray on the bench. "Later, maybe."

Felicity didn't try to sip her coffee. It looked too hot. "I'm not the gory type," she said mildly. "But I've liked Judd Almond's other books and thought I'd give this a try. His plots are always complex and so are his characters. He surprises me all the time, and I like that.''

''And what about this particular book?''

''So far, so good. It is a bit gory but I just skip the unpleasant parts.''

''Too bad,'' he said, ''that we can't do that in real life. Skip the unpleasant parts, I mean.''

''Like today?''

''Yeah. I must say this isn't the most pleasant of days.'' The warmth had gone from his voice, and he sounded detached. ''The rain's getting heavier by the minute.''

That's not what I meant, thought Felicity. And that's not what he'd originally meant either. But she'd be wise to let it ride. The weather was certainly atrocious, but this whole trip must be worse than unpleasant as far as he was concerned. It must be anathema to him...having to drive her to the funeral of a man he hated.

She tried a sip of her coffee and it had cooled enough to drink it. Mandy had closed her eyes and was slumped against her father, who was staring out the window. His gaze was unfocused; his face set in a frown.

He was wearing a black shirt with a pair of black dress pants. The shirt made his green eyes dark as midnight and it also accentuated the very faintest shadow of a mustache. He looked sexier than she'd ever seen him. Sexier than any other man she'd ever met.

Sexier than any man had a right to be.

She returned her attention to her book, but found herself unable to concentrate because all she could see on the page was the face of the man she'd grown to love.

*   *   *

"We're almost there, Jordan. Turn right along that side road."

Jordan made the turn and found they were on a paved lane. Slowing the car, he said, "How are you feeling?"

"Anxious. I'm not sure how Mom will be. Denny was her firstborn and he was her favorite."

Jordan stared ahead grimly. He didn't want to hear her talk of her brother. But at the same time, he knew this must be very difficult for her, and like it or not he did feel a strong sense of compassion for her.

"Mom knew he could slip away at any time but...well, that won't have made it any easier for her to bear. And she's already lost one son. This must be so hard for her."

"And for you." Though Jordan couldn't help feeling sorry for her, this was still the last place he wanted to be and once he'd dropped her off, he'd be out of there with the speed of light. But not to any beach, as Felicity had suggested the other day; the rain was still teeming down and showed no signs of letting up. "Your friend Hugh mentioned that you'd lost your twin brother. I can't imagine how that must have felt."

She didn't answer.

"I'm sorry," he muttered. "Hugh said you never talked about him. Forget I—"

"It felt, at first, and for many months, as if I was looking in a mirror for a reflection and seeing nothing, just an empty space. Then gradually, very gradually, an image started to form, but when it finally materialized, all I saw was...myself. Not Todd, as I'd been used to seeing all my life. Just me. On my own."

"Impossible to imagine, for anyone who hasn't lost a twin."

"It's been over two years," she said quietly. "The pain's still there, but it's not as sharp as it was in the beginning. Having Mandy in my life has helped enormously."

Mandy had fallen asleep on the drive down the island from Nanaimo. Now at mention of her name, she stirred. "Are we here, Fizzy?"

Felicity was glad of the interruption. Todd's death had shattered her and she'd always avoided talking about him, yet she'd just opened up to Jordan in a way she never had to anyone before. His understanding and empathy touched her, but she didn't want to become more vulnerable to him than she already was. She was emotionally unsteady today, because of the funeral, and she'd have to take care not to let her guard down. If he ever found out that she'd fallen in love with him, the situation they were already in would become untenable. And how would that affect Mandy?

"Fizzy?" Mandy tugged her sleeve. "Are we here?"

"Yes, darling." Felicity put an arm around her. "We're here."

Through the driving rain, the house loomed up ahead, a white, rambling two-storied building with dormer windows, lemon trim and a glassed-in front porch.

"Pretty place," Jordan murmured, negotiating his way among several cars parked randomly in a paved forecourt.

"Mom's pride and joy." Felicity's voice had softened. "She lives for home and family."

"Can I see?" Mandy's small fingers nimbly undid her seat belt so she could scramble up on the seat and look out. "Ooh, it is pretty! Is this where you used to live, Fizzy?"

An Important Message from the Editors

Dear Reader,

Because you've chosen to read one of our fine romance novels, we'd like to say "thank you!" And, as a special way to thank you, we've selected two more of the books you love so well, plus an exciting Mystery Gift, to send you absolutely FREE!

Please enjoy them with our compliments...

Pam Powers

P.S. And because we value our customers, we've attached something extra inside...

Peel off seal and place inside...

EDITOR'S FREE GIFT SEAL — THANK YOU

How to validate your Editor's
FREE GIFT
"Thank You"

1. Peel off gift seal from front cover. Place it in space provided at right. This automatically entitles you to receive 2 FREE BOOKS and a fabulous mystery gift.

2. Send back this card and you'll get 2 brand-new Harlequin Romance® novels. These books have a cover price of $3.99 each in the U.S. and $4.50 each in Canada, but they are yours to keep absolutely free.

3. There's no catch. You're under no obligation to buy anything. We charge nothing—ZERO—for your first shipment. And you don't have to make any minimum number of purchases—not even one!

4. The fact is, thousands of readers enjoy receiving their books by mail from the Harlequin Reader Service®. They enjoy the convenience of home delivery...they like getting the best new novels at discount prices BEFORE they're available in stores...and they love their *Heart to Heart* subscriber newsletter featuring author news, horoscopes, recipes, book reviews and much more!

5. We hope that after receiving your free books you'll want to remain a subscriber. But the choice is yours— to continue or cancel, any time at all! So why not take us up on our invitation, with no risk of any kind. You'll be glad you did!

6. Don't forget to detach your FREE BOOKMARK. And remember...just for validating your Editor's Free Gift Offer, we'll send you THREE gifts, *ABSOLUTELY FREE!*

GET A
FREE MYSTERY GIFT...

*SURPRISE MYSTERY GIFT COULD BE YOURS **FREE** AS A SPECIAL "THANK YOU" FROM THE EDITORS OF HARLEQUIN*

Visit us online at
www.eHarlequin.com

The Editor's "Thank You" Free Gifts Include:

- Two BRAND-NEW romance novels!
- An exciting mystery gift!

PLACE FREE GIFT SEAL HERE

$\mathcal{YES}!$ I have placed my Editor's "Thank You" seal in the space provided above. Please send me 2 free books and a fabulous mystery gift. I understand I am under no obligation to purchase any books, as explained on the back and on the opposite page.

386 HDL DNS9   **186 HDL DNSX**

(H-R-06/02)

FIRST NAME	LAST NAME

ADDRESS

APT.#	CITY

STATE/PROV.	ZIP/POSTAL CODE

Thank You!

BUSINESS REPLY MAIL
FIRST-CLASS MAIL   PERMIT NO. 717-003   BUFFALO, NY

POSTAGE WILL BE PAID BY ADDRESSEE

HARLEQUIN READER SERVICE
3010 WALDEN AVE
PO BOX 1867
BUFFALO NY 14240-9952

NO POSTAGE
NECESSARY
IF MAILED
IN THE
UNITED STATES

"Yes, I lived here until I went to art school when I was eighteen."

"I didn't know you studied art." Jordan drew the car to a halt and killed the engine. "Do you paint?"

"Not anymore. I went from there to specializing in design, which I loved, and then I became interested in quilting—I'd always enjoyed sewing. So—"

"So you ended up putting the two together. And making a living out of it. Clever girl."

"Not quite making a living at it, and that's why I ran my little day care, too. I loved looking after babies— and they sleep a lot so it used to work out well."

"But you stayed with Mandy after she was past the baby stage."

"How could I not?" she asked simply. "We'd grown so close I couldn't bear to part with her!"

"Fizzy!" Mandy tugged Felicity's sleeve again, this time more impatiently. "Come on, let's go in!"

Jordan said, "You and I aren't going in, Mandy. We're going to drop Felicity off and come back for her later. After the funeral reception's over."

"No!" Mandy clung indignantly to Felicity. "I'm staying with Fizzy!"

Felicity said, "I told you that you couldn't stay, sweetie. You and your daddy will come back for me—"

"Don't leave me!" Mandy shot her arms around Felicity's neck and caught her in a stranglehold. "Don't leave me, don't leave me…"

She sounded frantic. Almost hysterical.

"Felicity, just go." Jordan grasped his daughter firmly but gently and tried to pull her free. But she was having none of it. Her grip tightened, her cries became more and more desperate.

"No, no, no!" Her fragile little body arched taut as a bowstring. "Don't leave me again, you can't leave me again..." She began to sob, a heart-rending sound.

Jordan's frustrated glance met Felicity's anguished one as his further attempts to pry his daughter loose met with uncontrolled screams.

And then Mandy started to gag. He could see she was making herself sick.

What the hell was he going to—

"I'll have to take her in with me." Felicity had raised her voice to make herself heard over Mandy's gagging and the heavy drumming of rain on the car roof.

Hissing something under his breath, Jordan drew back. "OK. I guess we have no choice. She's making herself ill. In you go, then. What time should I come back?"

"No!" Mandy's eyes had a panicky expression as she gasped out the protest. "You have to come. too, Daddy!"

Felicity looked apologetically at Jordan. "I'm afraid you'll have to—"

"*It's out of the question.*"

Eyes appealing, she said, "I'll have to sit with the family during the church service but you can sit at the back with Mandy. As long as she can see me, as long as she can see that I'm not going to disappear again, she'll be fine—"

"Do you realize what you're *asking?*"

"Yes, of course I do!"

"It's too much."

Felicity was hugging Mandy close, caressing her back, trying to calm her down. "Then I've wasted my time coming, wasted your time, too. We might as well all go back to the mainland—''

"No. You should be here. Your mother needs you and you need to be here, too."

"But Mandy needs me. Just as much."

If he hadn't seen the tears welling up in her eyes, he might have tossed them both out of the car and taken off. But the tears undid him. He knew he had to put her feelings—and his daughter's welfare—before his own. Or he'd never forgive himself.

"All right." Had he ever before sounded so churlish? "OK. I'll do it. I'll stay."

Her look of gratitude was wasted on him. All he could think of, as she quieted Mandy down and brushed his daughter's tear-damp hair from her flushed cheeks, was that this woman had somehow suckered him into attending the funeral of her brother—a man who had not only cuckolded him but killed his wife.

The door of the sunporch burst open as they splashed their helter-skelter way across the forecourt and a pretty brunette beamed out at them, her hazel eyes alight.

"Felicity, at last! What a day!"

Inside the porch, with the door closed behind them, the rain battered down on the roof like nails from a gun.

Breathlessly, as she bent to take off Mandy's raincoat, Felicity said, "Sarah, this is Jordan Maxwell. Jordan, my sister, Sarah Matthews."

"Hi, Jordan, delighted to meet you. Let me take your jacket."

He shrugged it off and she shook it before hanging it on a coatrack.

Felicity hung up her coat and Mandy's and then

turned to give her sister a warm hug before saying, anxiously, "How's Mom?"

"Much as you'd expect. You'll see." Sarah looked down at Mandy who was clinging to Felicity's arm. "And this," she said gently, "must be Mandy." She crouched down. "Hi, Mandy. My little girl's about your age and she has nobody to play with. Would you like to come and meet her?"

Mandy hid her face in the skirt of Felicity's black dress.

Felicity stroked her head. "Maybe later, Mandy?"

Mandy peeked up at Sarah, but said not a word.

Sarah gave her another smile, before straightening. "You're coming to the funeral, Jordan?" Her gaze was direct.

Before he could answer, Felicity said, "Jordan was just going to drop me off but...Mandy didn't want me to leave her—"

"Felicity!" A shaky voice came from the interior doorway. "I didn't know you'd arrived."

They all turned toward the speaker, and Jordan saw a slim petite woman of around sixty, wearing something dark. Her blond hair was cut very short, with feathered bangs that set off neat features and lovely gray eyes.

This must be Felicity's mother, Jordan thought. And it occurred to him that this was exactly what Felicity would look like, thirty years down the road; a touch of silver in her hair, a few fine lines on her face, but still incredibly attractive.

Sarah said, "If you'll excuse me, everybody, I'll go help in the kitchen."

She took off, and as she did, Felicity said,

"Mom, this is Jordan Maxwell. And this—" she put

a hand gently on Mandy's head "—is his daughter, Mandy. Jordan, I'd like you to meet my mother, Adelaide Fairfax."

Adelaide Fairfax looked stunned. And then she swayed. She might have fallen if Felicity hadn't quickly put an arm around her for support.

"Mom, are you all right?" Felicity flashed an apologetic look at Jordan, before refocusing her attention on her mother. "I'm sorry, Mom. I didn't tell you Jordan was coming, I didn't think you'd need to know, as I wasn't planning on bringing him in. But…" She explained everything in shorthand form, while her mother kept her gaze averted from Jordan and fixedly on his daughter.

"I think," Adelaide whispered when Felicity finished, "that I need a little brandy."

Jordan felt he should say something. This situation, as impossible as it was for him, was even worse for this woman. Today she was burying the son she loved.

"Mrs. Fairfax, I regret—"

She closed her eyes and leaned into Felicity. "Take me up to my bedroom, dear. I need some time to be alone."

Felicity helped her mother upstairs, after throwing Jordan a distressed, "Thanks," when he took charge of Mandy.

As if her mother hadn't had enough to cope with, she reflected; she now had to cope with being reminded, on the day of her son's funeral, of the ignoble circumstances that had led to his death.

"I'm *really* sorry, Mom, that I had to bring Jordan in." She opened her mother's bedroom door. "There

was just no other way. I was so worried about Mandy,
she's been through so much already, and she became
hysterical at the prospect of being separated from me.
The only alternative was for me not to be here, but I
wanted you to have all your family with you today…what's left of it.''

Her mother pulled herself free as Felicity made to help
her onto the bed.

In a voice that trembled, she said, "I do have all my
remaining family here with me today. Thanks to you."

She had a strange, wild look in her eyes that alarmed
Felicity.

"Mom, won't you lie down? I think—"

"Get me that brandy. And one for yourself, too."

"You *know* I don't like brandy—"

The expression in her mother's eyes was one she'd
very rarely seen there; but it was one she *had* experienced before and she knew this was no time to disobey
an order.

When she came back upstairs, with two tots of brandy,
she found her mother standing exactly where she'd left
her.

"Here you are, Mom."

Her mother took the glass, took several sips, one
swiftly after another, till the glass was empty. She shud-
dered. "You now," she said.

What on earth was going on? Felicity took a cautious
sip, felt the alcohol burn her throat. Took another. And
then, after screwing up her nose, she drank the rest.

Her mother set both glasses on her dresser before turning again to Felicity. Her cheeks had two feverish
splotches, like crimson flags.

"Mom, what *is* it?"

"Felicity, when I said earlier that all the family were here, thanks to you, that's what I meant. All my family are here today. *Including Denny's daughter.*"

Felicity felt a pang of panic. Had her mother lost her mind? "Mom—" she reached out and grasped her mother's shoulders gently "—Denny didn't *have* any children."

"Oh, but he did, my darling. He had a daughter. A dear little girl. An adorable, beautiful little girl! And she's downstairs this very instant. With Jordan Maxwell. The man she believes to be her father."

"With…Jordan?" Felicity stared at her incredulously.

"Yes, dear. With Jordan."

"Mom, surely you're not saying—"

"Yes, Felicity, that is *exactly* what I'm saying." Joy shone through the tears welling up in her mother's eyes. "Denny's lawyer gave me a letter today, one that Denny had arranged three years ago to be given to me in case of his premature death. In it there is indisputable proof— DNA proof, my darling!—that Mandy Maxwell is Denny's daughter."

CHAPTER SEVEN

JORDAN stood in the front hall with Mandy, his gaze narrowed as he watched Felicity come slowly down the stairs.

She looked as if someone had run her through a wringer, her face white as a bleached sheet, her lips pressed together, her eyelashes wet with squeezed-out tears.

Mandy moved to the foot of the stairs. "What's wrong, Fizzy?"

"Nothing's wrong, darling." Felicity reached the foot of the stairs and sitting on the second bottom step, pulled Mandy over and held her close. "It's just," she said huskily, "that funerals make me very sad."

"I won't go away and leave you, Fizzy." Mandy's gaze was earnest. Her voice quivered as she added, "I *promise.*"

"Oh, darling, I know you won't!" Felicity kissed her brow. "And I'll never leave you. I love you so much."

Jordan felt his throat muscles tighten and ache. Darn it, why did women have to be so emotional!

"Felicity, is your mother OK?" He hadn't meant to sound so gruff and impatient.

She didn't look up, but bent her head over Mandy's and her long braid fell sideways over his daughter's shoulder. "She'll be fine." The words were muffled. "She just needed a few minutes by herself—"

"Still here?" Sarah swept through from a passage beyond the stairs, bearing a tray steaming with fragrant savoury snacks. "Time for something to eat," she said, making for a closed door on the right. "Something light, to tide the family over till after the funeral. Felicity, you can give me a hand. Jordan, would you open this door?"

When Jordan opened the door, a hubbub of voices flowed into the hall. He stepped aside to let Sarah pass, with Felicity and Mandy at her heels.

Reluctantly, he followed them, and had just entered the large airy room when he heard someone say, from behind, "Excuse me!"

He turned, to see a young female with spiky burgundy hair, and a coffee carafe in each hand. She smiled. "Hi, you must be Jordan. I'm Gigi, Felicity's baby sister! Pleased to meet you."

He nodded. "Hi."

With a backward kick of her ankle boot, she flicked the door shut. "Find a seat," she said over her shoulder as she threaded her way among the several people standing around, deep in conversation. "Someone will feed you!"

Felicity moved to his side. "Jordan, I know this is uncomfortable for you—"

"I'll survive." He looked down at her but she was looking at Mandy—who was in turn staring at a red-headed little girl holding a doll's tea party in the bay window area. His gaze returned to Felicity, and he saw she was still looking at Mandy...but with a piercing intensity that puzzled him. She could have been studying a stranger.

Suddenly Mandy announced, "I'm hungry."

Felicity started, as if she'd been a thousand miles away. "What did you say, sweetie?"

"I'm hungry."

"That's not surprising," Felicity said. "You've hardly eaten a thing all day. But first I'll introduce you and your—" She wiped a hand over her brow, and he saw a glimmer of perspiration. "First I'll introduce you and your father around and then—"

"I don't want to be introduced around." Jordan knew he sounded grumpy as a bear with an ear abscess. "I just want to find a quiet corner and be left alone."

"OK, if you and Mandy want to sit over there, on that love seat, I'll bring you—"

"No," Mandy said. "I want to go over *there.*" She pointed to the red-haired child. "She's having a party. And she has cookies."

"You want to play with Hannah? Oh, she'll love that!"

"You come, too, Fizzy."

"I have to help my sisters…but…." She looked up at Jordan and he felt a jolt of alarm when he noticed the haunted expression in her eyes. "Jordan, will you take Mandy over to meet Hannah? I'll bring you coffee and a couple of sausage rolls."

And with that, she fled—there was no other word for it—to join her sisters who were busy with the food, at a gateleg table at the far side of the room.

"Fliss, the man's to die for!" Sarah rolled her eyes. "Now I know why you haven't been home since you moved to Deerhaven. Jordan Maxwell can put his shoes under my bed any time he wants!"

"Better not let Brett hear you say that!" Felicity replied, trying to sound amused as she referred to Sarah's husband. She poured coffee into a mug. "Gigi, put a couple of sausage rolls on a plate for Jordan."

"Are you getting it off with the guy?" Gigi's burgundy-lipsticked mouth curled in a mischievous smile.

Felicity frowned at her young sister. "Don't be crude."

Gigi put three sausage rolls on a plate. "Sorry. He *is* drop-dead gorgeous, though...but he looks a bit surly."

"He's probably feeling surly," Sarah said, "because of the situation. He can't want to be here!"

"He doesn't." Felicity slid the mug of coffee over the table to Gigi. "If you want to go flirt with him here's your chance."

Gigi grinned. "Hey, an offer I can't refuse!" She pranced away towards Jordan, who was slouched in an armchair by the girls, who seemed to have become instant friends.

Felicity was relieved to see that Mandy was chomping on a cookie, but when her gaze moved to Jordan, a feeling of panicky desperation churned her stomach.

Her mother had given her an ultimatum.

She had to tell Jordan that Mandy wasn't his child.

And if she didn't, her mother would...

Because Adelaide Fairfax wanted her granddaughter.

"She's Denny's daughter!" her mother had cried. "She should be here. With me. This is her family home!"

Felicity's head was spinning. "No, she *can't* be Denny's." She laughed, slightly hysterically. "For heaven's sake, Mom, Denny didn't even *meet* Marla Maxwell till just a few months before the accident!"

"That's what everyone believed. But do you think it was a mere coincidence that the woman hired you to look after her baby? Out of all the possible baby-sitters in the Lower Mainland, didn't it ever occur to you to wonder why she chose you?''

"No! She said she'd been referred to me by a friend whose infant son I'd looked after—"

"*Denny* was the one who chose you, Fliss. When she discovered she was pregnant, Marla didn't want the baby but Denny—well, he didn't want a family but he wanted that baby to be born and—oh, darling, we can't go into this right now." Adelaide reached to the dresser for a tissue, and wiped her eyes. "But believe me, I have proof—DNA results from when Mandy was an infant. There's absolutely no doubt about it."

Felicity felt tears welling up. "Oh, Mom, Jordan loves her so much, she means *everything* to him. This would kill him if he ever found out."

"But of course he's going to find out!" Her mother sounded appalled. "I haven't mentioned it to anyone else yet, he at least deserves to be the first to know. But Felicity, you must tell him! And you must tell him soon! I absolutely insist!"

This, Felicity thought as she watched Gigi perch confidently on the arm of Jordan's chair and bat her eyelashes at him, had to be the worst day of her life.

What on earth was she going to do?

Denny was Mandy's father. The test results, which Adelaide had shown her—and which were now tucked in her own handbag!—proved it beyond a shadow of a doubt.

But by telling Jordan the truth, Felicity knew she would break his heart. And might well destroy him.

"Fliss, if you take around the cream and sugar, I'll serve the coffee." Sarah's voice cut through Felicity's fog of despair. "Our younger sister," she added wryly, "has deserted us in favor of the surly Heathcliff. Poor man. Fliss, surely he's done his bit by acting as your chauffeur. Wouldn't he prefer to stay here, at the house, while you go to the funeral?"

"I hadn't thought of that. But it would be up to Mandy. I doubt she'll allow me to go without her. She's so very insecure..."

"I'd leave Hannah for company but she did love her uncle Denny and she wants to come with Brett and me."

It occurred to Felicity that Mandy should surely be attending her father's funeral. But she couldn't cope with that thought; she was finding it hard enough to cope with the fact that Denny actually *was* the child's father.

"I'll check with Mandy," she said. "See what she says."

Surprisingly, Mandy was quite happy to stay. "As long as I can play with Hannah's dolls. Can I, Hannah?"

"Sure. And my tea set. And anything in my bedroom!"

So it was all settled.

And when Felicity left for the funeral, her last sight of Jordan and Mandy was of the two of them, standing together at the sitting room window, watching through the lashing rain as she was driven away in a black limousine.

During the reception that followed the funeral, Felicity whispered goodbyes to her mother and the rest of the family before she slipped away with Jordan and Mandy.

Her mother hadn't tried to keep her.

"It will be easier for me," Adelaide said to Felicity, "if I don't get to know Jordan Maxwell. That way, if we end up in court, it won't be so awkward for either of us.''

The prospect of a court battle, with her mother and Jordan fighting for possession of Mandy, drove Felicity into even deeper despair.

And Jordan couldn't help noticing her black mood.

"I hadn't realized," Jordan said as they approached Nanaimo, "that today would be *quite* so harrowing for you."

No, reflected Felicity, nor had she. She'd known it would be a difficult day, but she hadn't anticipated that during it, she'd have to hear such devastating news.

She glanced around at Mandy, who was asleep on the back seat. My niece, she thought, with a shiver of awe. My own flesh and blood. *Denny's* baby. No wonder she'd always felt such a close tie with her, ever since she'd taken over her care when Mandy was just a scrap of a thing, with pink cheeks and a mass of wheat-colored hair—

"Felicity!"

She started, and jerked her head around to look at Jordan. "What?"

She saw his jaw tighten, and after scrutinizing her sharply, he checked in the rearview mirror, then swung the car off the road and parked on the gravel shoulder.

"You look all-in," he said. "And you don't even seem to hear me. I said your name three times! Is there something wrong? I mean...*really wrong*...more than the funeral."

He sounded harsh, but his eyes were dark with concern.

"I'm fine—" The words came out chokingly. And

before she knew it, and to her utter dismay, she started to weep.

She heard the snap of his seat belt and then she was in his arms. Her face was pressed to his black shirt, her tears spilling into it. Oh, Jordan, she beseeched silently, what am I going to do?

"Hush," he whispered, and gently ran a hand up and down her back, as he held her close. "Here's what we'll do. I'm going to drive us to my sister's place. It's not too many miles from here. And I'm going to have her cook you a hot nourishing meal while you sit with your feet up. We're not going on any ferry until I think you're ready to walk without falling flat on your face."

She looked up at him, her cheeks wet with tears. "We can't just drop by on someone and she might not even be home and—"

"Ssh." His knuckles were tender as he used them to wipe away her tears. "My sister's not someone, she's Alice, and she'll be home. She's nine months pregnant and not about to be gallivanting around at this stage in the game."

Their eyes met, and...held. Green, his were so green. So dark with intent.

She couldn't move. She had no will to resist. She was aware of nothing, but the green of his eyes. And then came the brush of his fingertips as he slid them to her nape, the quiver of a pulse as he caressed her skin, the sharp intake of breath—her own—as he lowered his head and claimed her lips in a kiss so sensual, so passionate, so masterful, it enslaved her as surely as if he'd bound her with chains.

She melted into it, not wanting this perfect moment to end. She knew she could never let him kiss her again.

Not that he would *want* to kiss her again. Once he knew the truth about Mandy, any chance of having even a friendship with him would be shattered.

When he drew back, his eyes were shadowed with emotion.

"That," he said softly, "was—"

"A mistake." She sounded panicky.

"Our only mistake—" he ran a fingertip over her upper lip "—was that we ever thought it would be a mistake."

"Jordan—"

"I know what you're going to say. If you hadn't been so 'down', you'd never have let it happen. I know. And I didn't mean to take advantage of you. I do apologize for that. But although I apologize for the timing, I'm not going to apologize for the kiss. I did a lot of thinking, when you were at the funeral, and I realized how wrong it was of me, and how unfair, to have let my bitterness at Denny seep out to include you...and your family. They're good people. I could see that today. I've blamed Denny for everything bad that happened, but in the same way, your family could have blamed Marla for—"

"They didn't, Jordan. Nobody ever blamed her—"

"Let me finish. They could have held Marla responsible for everything. Whether they did or not, your family—particularly your sisters—treated me today with courtesy, which is more than can be said for the way I've treated you. Can you find it in your heart to forgive me? Can we make a fresh start? Can we be on the same team? It would mean so much to me—"

"Daddy?" Mandy's drowsy voice came from the back seat. "Are we on the ferry?"

"Just a minute, honey. *Felicity?*"

She pulled back, and with a trembling hand, brushed a stray strand of hair behind her ear. Confusion made her head pound. It would be a lie to say yes, they'd be on the same team. Family loyalty would surely give her no choice but to be on her mother's team. But now wasn't the time to tell Jordan any of that. "We can talk later," she said. And telling no fib, she added, "I feel...wobbly right now."

"Daddy!" Mandy kicked his seat. "What's *happening?*"

Jordan touched the back of his hand to Felicity's cheek, the gesture reassuring. "OK, we'll talk later."

Then he set the car in motion.

"We're going to the ranch," he said to Mandy. "Fizzy's not too well. I think—I hope—that she'll feel a lot better after your aunt Alice has given her something lovely to eat."

But Alice McTaggart wasn't at home.

"She's at a baby shower," her husband Dermid told Jordan when he welcomed them at his alpaca ranch. "Too bad you've missed her. The only night for weeks that she's been away from the place." He brought them into a slate-floored entry where Jordan relieved Felicity of her coat while Dermid helped Mandy with hers.

"And how are ye, my wee lass?" he asked his niece, a burr in his voice and a warmth in his eyes—eyes that were the same golden-brown as the finest malt whiskey.

"I'm very well, thank you." Mandy kept close to Felicity.

"Certainly looking a lot better than last time we met! And who, may I enquire, is this fine lady?" His shrewd once-over made a weary Felicity straighten her spine.

"She's Fizzy, Uncle Dermid. She's in our *family*."

"I'm pleased to make your acquaintance, Fizzy." Grinning, Dermid stuck out a big hand and hers became lost in it. He didn't let go, but held on to it while he peered into her eyes. Then he gave her the same slanting smile he'd given his niece, and one equally warm. "Aye," he said. "You're looking a wee bit wabbit, but you'll do."

Felicity blinked. "Wabbit?"

Wryly, Jordan said, "It's the Scottish equivalent of 'wiped'. And she *is* exhausted, you red-haired heathen. Can you fix her up with a plate of something hot?"

"Och, I do believe we have some haggis, now, in the freezer, left over from the last Burns' supper."

"Oh." Embarrassed, Felicity wrinkled her nose. "I...I'm afraid I don't like haggis."

Jordan chuckled. "OK, Dermid, you can drop the act. He's just kidding, Felicity. His accent's as phony as the Loch Ness monster. He may have been born on the other side of the pond but he's as Canadian as they come."

Dermid's ruggedly hacked face creased in a wide smile. "Right," he said. "No haggis. But let's get you all into the kitchen and see what we can rustle up."

Felicity felt Mandy's hand creep into hers as they all made their way into the country kitchen, with its well-worn plank floor, rustic-looking pine cupboards, and harvest table with eight ladder-backed chairs.

"Have a seat," Dermid said, before crossing to the fridge. As Felicity sat down, she noticed that his head almost hit the clothes-pulley that hung high from the ceiling. He must be well over six feet. And powerfully built. But his hair wasn't red, as Jordan had proclaimed it to be. It was a glorious auburn-brown, rich and wavy.

"How's Alice?" Jordan tilted back his chair.

Dermid took out a couple of lidded containers and swung the fridge door shut with his knee. "Everything was fine at her last checkup." He glanced at Felicity. "How about this?" He held up the containers. "Chicken and leek soup, and a spot of veggie lasagna to follow?"

"That would be wonderful," Felicity said. "But I hate to put you to all this bother—"

"Hey!" He shook his head. "No problem. Any friend of Jordan's is a friend of mine." He winked at his niece. "And ditto, any friend of Mandy's."

Mandy giggled.

As Dermid took the lids off and crossed to the microwave, Felicity sensed Jordan's eyes on her. Unable to help herself, she looked across the table at him.

"Are we?" he said quietly. "Friends?"

How could she say no, with those beguilingly beautiful green eyes seducing her into saying yes? He didn't know the heartbreak that lay ahead of him. Surely the least she could do, at this moment, was to go along with his wishes.

"Yes," she said. "If that's what you want."

But for how long *would* he want her as a friend? He'd finally managed to accept her for the person she was, and not "Denny Fairfax's sister." But when he learned he wasn't Mandy's father, when he learned the full extent of his wife's betrayal and the part Denny had played in it, she knew one thing for sure: he'd hate the Fairfax name—and everyone associated with it—as he'd never hated it before.

She felt as if her heart was breaking. In the car, he had kissed her with such tenderness. If things had been different, was it possible they might have become much more than friends?

But there was no point in even thinking about that. It wasn't going to happen.

It was more important to think of how he was going to feel about Mandy once he found out she was Denny's daughter.

Felicity hunched over a little as her stomach twisted. She couldn't bear it if he rejected the child—

"Felicity, are you all right?"

She dragged herself from her bleak reflections. Managing a smile, she responded to Jordan's question.

"I'll be fine," she said. "Once I've eaten." She turned her smile to Dermid, who had set four bowls on the table and was ladling steaming soup into them. "Mmm," she said, and put all the enthusiasm she could into her voice. "That does smell delicious!"

It was, indeed, delicious. As was the lasagna. And after they'd all eaten, Mandy asked if Dermid would take her to see the animals.

"It's a bit wild out there," he said. "Rain's still lashing down. You think you're up to it?"

Mandy's nod was vigorous. "I'll wrap up well. Please, Uncle Dermid?"

"Sure."

"Do you still have Angel?" Mandy wriggled off her chair, her face alight. "And Primrose and Shadow?"

"Yup, all still here." Dermid rose from the table. "Let's go. And we'll leave Fizzy and your Daddy to do the dishes! How does that sound?"

She carried her lasagna plate over to the counter. "Sounds good to me!"

"Unless you want to come with us?" Dermid threw Felicity and Jordan a questioning look.

Jordan said, "No, we'll stay here. OK, Felicity?"

"Yes, I'd rather not go out."

Dermid and Mandy left, and Jordan said, "I'll wash." He began clearing dishes. "I'll dry, too, if you're not up to it."

"I'm fine now. I'll dry."

After they'd cleared the table, Felicity wiped it off before taking a dish towel from a hook glued to the side of the fridge. "You could pop the plates in the dishwasher."

"Nah." He ran hot water into the sink, adding a squirt of dishwashing liquid. "There's something companionable about doing dishes together. All these modern appliances may make life easier, but they also make it more clinical. Less intimate. Some things are better done the old-fashioned way." He turned off the tap, and sank several dishes into the frothy water.

"Even if the old-fashioned way isn't always the more efficient way?"

"Yeah, even if." He rinsed plates, one by one, and set them on the plastic rack. "Take making beds, for instance. Most people use duvets now, so they just air them in the morning, toss them back onto the bed again at night."

"What's wrong with that?"

"Nothing. But beds and dishes are best done by two people. Take the marriage bed. It may have taken longer to make a bed when blankets and quilts were the thing, but still, when a couple—a couple in love, that is!— made the bed together in the morning it probably ended up, oftener than not, in some not-very-clinical fun!"

He glanced at Felicity. She appeared to be concentrating on the dish she was drying, but she was blushing. And she looked endearingly sweet.

Something inside him melted as he looked at her and remembered the kiss in the car. It had been glorious. He hadn't realized, till that very moment, that all along, even when he'd refused to admit it to himself, he'd been falling in love with her. And with every passing moment, the feeling deepened. He was a goner. Head over heels. Not *falling* in love, but already in love with her.

He took the plate from her one hand, the towel from her other. And as she glanced at him, startled, questioning, he put his arms around her, pulled her close and kissed her. Again.

This time, no holds barred.

He felt every curve of her body pliant against his, felt his own body's instant response. He wanted her. More than anything he'd ever wanted in his life.

And she was kissing him back with a desperation that fueled his desire. She pressed herself to him, arched up against him, and with a whimper in her throat, opened her lips to him at the first touch of his tongue.

She tasted of the strawberries they'd had for dessert. She smelled of wildflowers and summer rain. And she felt, in his arms, like a gift straight from heaven, all peaceful and perfect and pure.

Peaceful. Odd that he should think that, when every nerve in his body was aquiver with need. But she did fill him with peace, the first peace his soul had experienced in years.

Trembling, he drew back, and through a mist of tears looked down at her innocent face. Her cheeks were wet...with tears, too? And her gray eyes were hazed as

they searched his...hazed with wonder...shaded with
uncertainty.

She was so vulnerable.

He must never hurt her again.

He *would* never hurt her again.

He must go carefully, so as not to frighten her. He
yearned to tell her of his love, but it was too soon. Far
too soon for her to believe he could have gone from hate
to love in such a short time.

Instead, he eased her gently from him.

"I told you," he teased, "that the old way of doing
dishes was better. And now—" he added, his eyes twinkling, his smile amused "—haven't I just proved my
point?"

CHAPTER EIGHT

FELICITY didn't for one moment believe Jordan had kissed her just to prove his point. He'd wanted her every bit as much as she wanted him. Even several hours later, as they drove up the hill to Deerhaven, she could still feel the imprint of his hard pressure against her and remember the charge of excitement that had sizzled between them.

She must never let him kiss her again. Besotted as she was, she might surrender completely to him, and she must avoid that at all costs. Once he learned the truth about Mandy, he would surely never forgive himself if he'd slept with Denny Fairfax's sister.

Now, as he slowed the car in the forecourt, she felt her stomach muscles clench into a knot. She loved him so very much. How could she bear to see him hurt? And yet, she was the one who had to do it.

If she didn't, her mother would.

"Please give me time, Mom," she'd begged. "I'll have to wait till...till the right moment presents itself."

"Don't take too long." Her mother had been pale but determined. "I can't wait to have Denny's daughter here, where she belongs. And if he fights me for her—"

"He may not want her now," Felicity had said tearfully. "But despite that, he'll be so devastated he may battle you in court just to get back at Denny...and the rest of us."

"Either way," her mother said, "I won't rest till

Mandy's in our family where she belongs. When I saw her, I just wanted to take her in my arms and tell her I'm her grandma and never let her go. Have you any idea what this means to me? To have lost Denny but then to discover that he's left this darling little girl?''

''Mom, *please* don't do or say anything today that would give Jordan any hint that—''

''Don't worry. Difficult as it will be, I won't. But Felicity, you have to *tell* the man! And soon.''

Stifling a deep sigh, Felicity gathered up her purse as Jordan pulled the car to a halt and killed the engine.

Mandy, who had been dozing in the back seat, surfaced.

''Daddy, where are we? Are we still on the ferry?''

He glanced around and shook his head. ''No, honey, we're not still on the ferry.'' He moved his gaze to Felicity and added, with a warm and tender smile that overturned her heart, ''We're home.''

The peace that Jordan had felt when he kissed Felicity in his sister's kitchen hadn't lasted. And he knew why.

Felicity was avoiding him.

She went out of her way to keep out of his way. And he could only deduce that he'd scared her off. His kiss had been too soon. Too passionate. Too intimate.

Yet she'd been as involved in it as he had been, her lips as soft and receptive as her body.

And the chemistry between them had blown him away. She *must* have felt it, too! Was *that* what had alarmed her?

A week had passed since their trip to the island, and during that week the only time she'd sought him out was to remind him that they needed to go shopping for clothes for Mandy.

This Friday afternoon was the first time he'd found himself free, and he'd picked Felicity and his daughter up from Deerhaven at two o'clock. Mandy was in a sunny mood that matched the day, and Felicity appeared to be less remote than usual—perhaps because she knew that with Mandy around, he wasn't likely to make any "moves" on her.

"So," he said, as they left Deerhaven, "Where are we headed?"

"There's a new children's store in Dundarave," Felicity said. "Anna's Place. Shall we give it a try?"

They drove down the hill to the village, and after parking, they walked along to Anna's Place. The store still smelled of fresh paint, and was jam-packed with attractively designed children's clothes. And before very long, with the help of Anna herself, Mandy was nicely kitted out.

Jordan paid the bill at the counter, while Felicity took charge of the several packages and Mandy danced around in front of a mirror, admiring her new pair of sandals.

Anna glanced at the signature on his credit card before handing the card back. "Thank you, Mr. Maxwell." As he slid the card into his wallet, she turned to Felicity. "Your daughter's charming, Mrs. Maxwell. And she looks so *very* like you, with her beautiful blond hair and lovely smile."

Till that moment, Felicity had seemed to be having fun. Now Jordan saw dismay flit over her face. Had it upset her, to be called Mrs. Maxwell? He saw she was about to correct Anna, but before she could, he put an arm around her and with a pleasant, "Thank you, Anna, for your help," he ushered her and Mandy out to the street.

"No need," he said, "to let that embarrass you. It was a natural mistake for her to think you were my wife."

She said nothing. But she still seemed distressed. So he said lightly, in an attempt to divert her, "I'd never noticed before, but you and Mandy do resemble each other—besides the blond hair, you both have gray eyes...and the lovely smile Anna mentioned. Maybe—" he tried to make a joke of it "—it's the same as with dogs and their owners. They do tend to look like each other after a while!"

Her smile was taut. "So they say."

They'd reached the car, and he opened the trunk. As Felicity dropped the packages in, Mandy said, "Daddy, can we have an ice cream now and go down to the beach?"

Before he could respond, Felicity said quickly, "Your father has to go back to work, sweetie."

There she was again, trying to dodge him.

"It's OK." He closed the trunk and held out a hand to his daughter. "I'm not in that much of a rush."

"Goody!" Mandy grabbed his thumb and slipping a hand into Felicity's, she tugged them up the sidewalk. "Let's go get the ice cream first. What kind do you want, Fizzy? I'm going to have peppermint with chunky chocolate chips!"

Jordan paid for their cones and then they all walked down 25th Street, and across the railway tracks. As they wandered over the grassy area above the beach, Mandy said, "You have to lick real quick or it melts, right, Daddy?"

"Right you are." He glanced at Felicity and was just in time to see her run the tip of her tongue up her vanilla ice cream to the peak. "How're you doing, Felicity?"

Without looking at him, she said, "Fine, thanks. This is lovely, Zanre's really do make the best ice cream, don't they!" Then she ran her tongue around the rim of the cone, catching a dribble of melted ice cream, as if that were the one and only thing she was interested in at this moment.

"Did I tell you," he asked, as Mandy skipped on ahead, "How pretty you're looking today?"

Her cheeks flushed. "It's just an old sundress," she said, and shrugged. "Nothing special—"

"I wasn't talking about the dress—although that shade of blue is lovely on you. I was talking about *you*."

"Oh." Her flush deepened. "Then…thank you."

But the compliment had obviously frightened her off, because before he had time to draw breath, she'd hurried on ahead to catch up with Mandy—leaving him frustrated.

When they reached the beach, which was haphazardly strewn with giant logs, Mandy raced for one that was flat on top.

"Let's sit here!" she called. And perching on it, she ordered, "You on this side, Fizzy, and Daddy, you on my other side."

They sat in the sunshine, licking their ice cream. Mandy was last to finish, and when she'd delicately crunched the point of her cone, she jumped off the log.

"I'm going down to paddle!" Plumping her little bottom down on the sand, she ripped off her new sandals.

Getting up, Felicity said, "I'll come with you—"

But Mandy ran toward the water, yelling back, "No, *stay* there with Daddy, I want you both to *watch!*"

Jordan saw Felicity hesitate.

"Sit down," he said. And added, in a teasing tone, "I'm not going to bite you!"

She turned to look down at him, and he was shocked to see an anguished expression in her eyes. But in a flash it was gone, and he had to wonder if it had just been a trick of the light.

"No," she said, "I'm sure you're not."

She sat down...but left a space between them.

He slid over to sit next her, so close his arm brushed hers. Her skin felt soft and warm. He had no desire to *bite* her, but he did ache to kiss her, to kiss her cheek, and feel the silk of it against his lips.

"Why," he asked softly, "have you been avoiding me?"

A seagull swooped by, screaming like a startled baby.

She followed its flight and he saw a faint movement in her throat as she swallowed.

"I don't want to be in your way," she said, her voice so soft he could scarcely hear it over the sound of Mandy's gleeful laughter as she danced over the sand, trying not to get wet as white-capped wavelets played games with her feet.

"Why do you think you'd be in my way?" he asked.

"When you're home, I feel you should be spending your spare time with Mandy, not with me. She needs you."

He paused for a beat. "And *you* don't?"

She turned to him, her eyes pleading. "You mustn't—"

"And *you* don't?" Steadily, he rode over her protest. "I think you need me every bit as much as I need you. And I swear you have nothing to fear from me. My intentions are strictly—"

She surged to her feet. "I forgot, I have to go to the bank. I'll pop up there now, so you won't have to hang around waiting for me, on our way home. I'll be back right away."

With a defeated sigh, Jordan got up and watched, as she flitted off up the beach like an elusive blue butterfly.

In the days that followed, work kept him busy and his hours became more erratic than ever. Even so, he couldn't help noticing that on the occasions when he did see Felicity, she seemed increasingly edgy and distracted.

He put it down to the fact that she'd just lost her brother. And he realized he had to give her space, and time, to get over her loss.

So despite his growing love for her, he didn't push.

But he worried about her.

Then one night, on arriving home very late and seeing her sewing room light was still on, he decided to have a talk with her. Stopping outside her door, he heard the whirr of her sewing machine. When he knocked, it stopped.

Silence fell.

He knocked again.

After a few moments, the door opened and she appeared.

When she saw him standing there, she lifted her hand nervously to her braid which lay like a rope of gleaming gold over the yoke of her fuchsia silk robe.

"I hadn't realized it was so late." Apology shadowed her eyes. "Was the noise of the sewing machine bothering you?"

"No, I just got home. I need to talk to you."

"Can't it wait till morning?"

"No. May I come in?"

With obvious reluctance, she stepped back.

He walked past her, into the room.

"What are you sewing?" He went to have a look at what she'd been working on and saw it was a patchwork quilt, with twenty blocks, each one depicting a nursery rhyme or fairy tale character.

"It's for Mandy's bed," she said. "I started it ages ago, but because it's to be a surprise, I've had to work on it when she wasn't around, so it's taken me a while to get it finished."

"It's finished now?"

"I was just putting the final touches to it when you knocked." She sliced off the threads which still attached it to the sewing machine needle, and sweeping up the quilt, shook it out and draped it over an armchair. Scrutinizing it, she said, "I hope she'll like it."

"How could she not? It's a work of art. And I'm sure a lot of love went into every single stitch."

"It did. She's the sweetest little girl in the world."

When he heard the catch in her voice, he yearned to take her in his arms. But he warned himself to tread carefully, he mustn't frighten her off again.

"She is," he said. "And she's the luckiest little girl, too, having you to care for her."

"No, I'm the lucky one. She means *everything* to me."

"You mean that, don't you! It awes me, Felicity—"

"What does?"

"That you have the capacity for that kind of love for a child who isn't your own. I know I don't. Maybe it's a matter of pride. Maybe it's because the male of the species has the responsibility for ensuring the continuity of the bloodline. Or maybe it's just something lacking in *me!* Whatever. I'm not capable of that kind of love…but you are. And because you are, Mandy is *truly* blessed."

"You said you wanted to talk to me." Her eyes had taken on a strained expression. "What was it about?"

"Let's sit down."

She hesitated, and taking her hand, he led her over to the green love seat. Sitting down, he patted the cushion beside him.

Still, she hesitated.

"I've told you before," he reminded her, "that I don't bite!"

"It's just that…well, I'm in my robe and it's not very proper for you to be in my room at this time of night, under the circumstances."

"And what," he asked, "*are* the circumstances?"

"Well, you're my employer and—"

"Uh-uh. We're family, you and I…and as I recall, you were the one who insisted on that! Am I right?"

"Yes, but—"

"No buts. Now, sit down, before I pull you down. And if I do, I promise you that you'll end up on my knee!"

Flushing, she sat, but kept as far away as she could…which wasn't too far, since it was a small love seat.

"OK." He stretched out his long legs in front of him on the carpet. "Are you ready?"

"For...what?"

"What I'm going to ask you."

'Yes, I'm ready."

"You have to look at me when I'm talking to you."

Her shoulders tensed, but she did turn to him. Her eyes were wary. "What?"

"I want to know why you're always running from me."

"I'm not—"

"Have I done something to offend you?"

"Of course not. If you had, I'd have told you. You must know by now that I can speak up for myself!"

"Then why have you been so...detached? I know that losing your brother must have upset you...but you're not this way with Mandy, nor with Lacey when she calls...nor even with the postman! So what else can I do but conclude it's personal. Between you and me."

She fiddled with her watch. She chewed her lip. Then she fidgeted with the lapel of her robe. Finally, with obvious unwillingness, she said, "You're right. I *have* been avoiding you. But...as for the reason...it's something I don't want to talk about. At least, not just yet."

"But why? You know, it really does help to open up and—"

"No. I'm not ready. But I will tell you, I promise. And I won't put it off much longer."

"Can't you tell me now?"

"I'm not ready."

He was more puzzled now than he'd been before he asked the question. And a heckuva lot more frustrated. But he could see she wasn't about to change her mind.

"OK," he said. "You give me no choice but to wait. But do you have to be so remote in the meantime? Can't we be friends while you're sorting out whatever it is you have to sort out? Don't you *want* to be friends?"

"Yes, of course I want us to be friends, but—"

"So you do *like* me?"

"Yes." The word came out raggedly. "Yes, of course I like you."

"Can I dare ask if you do a little more than like me?"

She turned away.

He caught her, made her turn back. Then framing her face with both hands, he said, "How much more?"

"Don't look at me like that. You're making me..." Her voice trailed away in a tiny whimper.

"Making you what? Fall in love with me?"

Her eyes were anguished. But the anguish couldn't hide the ache of wanting in the beautiful gray depths.

Hope flared up inside him. "Are you?" he asked, hardly daring to believe. "Falling in love...?"

She looked at him with the expression of someone drowning, going under for the third time and too far gone to look for help. "No," she whispered. "Not falling in love. I'm already in love with you and have been ever since—"

He didn't let her finish. Blindly, he claimed her mouth with his own and felt his heart sing when after a shivery sigh, she returned his kiss with a frantic desperation that matched his own.

Hauling her onto his lap, he held her so close he felt the breathless rise and fall of her breasts.

All his pent-up longing went into the kiss; and when finally he drew back to gaze upon her flushed face, he thought this must be as close to heaven as a man could get.

"I love you so much." He kissed her parted lips, a gentler, more tender kiss this time. "I know it's only a few weeks since we met, but I feel as if I've known you forever." He saw tiny flecks of white in her irises, like miniature snowflakes. "Yet there are still so very many things left to find out about you. And my darling, I want to spend the rest of my life with you. I want to m—"

She pressed the fingertips of her right hand against his lips. "No," she whispered urgently. "Don't..."

He drew her fingers down. "You can't stop me, Felicity. You love me, you've admitted it. And I'm crazy about you. I'm asking you to marry me, my darling. I want to look after you, and love you, for the rest of our lives."

She uttered a sound like a sob. "I can't. I can't marry you—"

"Why not?"

"I...just can't."

"No reason?"

She put a hand on the arm of the love seat and pushed herself up, as stiffly as someone who had aged twenty years overnight. "You'll know the reason, once I tell you what it is. I'll eventually tell you."

"But after you tell me," he said, getting up, "then will you let me ask the question again?"

Clasping her arms around herself, she nodded. "Oh, yes. You can ask it again...if you still want to."

Their voices must have disturbed Mandy because all of a sudden, he heard her wail, "Fizzy!"

Felicity made to step around him, but he stopped her.

"I'll attend to her," he said. "You get yourself off to

bed. I'm not going to pressure you any more just now, my darling. But I promise you, that whatever it is you have to tell me, I'll be ready with my question right after.''

Felicity did go to bed right away, but she didn't sleep— not right away, and not for a very long time.

How could she, with Jordan's proposal still ringing in her ears?

It should have been the happiest night of her life; instead it was the opposite. And she couldn't let the present situation continue much longer. It wasn't fair to her mother. Or to any of them. She had to tell Jordan that Denny was Mandy's father. And then all hell would probably break loose.

What was the worst possible scenario?

She got out of bed and stepped over to the window. Holding aside the drapes, she looked out wearily into a pink-streaked dawn.

The worst possible scenario was that Jordan would tell her to get out of his house...and take Denny's daughter with her.

Tears filled her eyes at the prospect. Tears not for herself, but for the man she loved and for the little girl he so adored.

Jordan had gone to the office before Felicity and Mandy arrived downstairs in the morning.

He had left a note, propped against the coffeemaker:

To my two best girls
    Have a wonderful day!

XXXXXX

"What does it say, Fizzy?" Mandy had just let RJ out for his morning prowl; now she edged onto her chair.

Felicity read the note to her. And added, "He sends kisses."

"What are we going to do today?" Mandy asked.

"What would you like to do?"

Before Mandy could answer, the phone rang. The caller was Lacey.

"I just got back from Accra," Jordan's sister said. "And I'm home—I hope!—for a whole week! I have something for Mandy, can I pop around this morning?"

"We'd love to see you, Lacey. We're just about to have breakfast, and we haven't planned our day yet, so let's do something together."

"Jordan's out?"

"Yes, he's already gone to the office."

"Good. I have something for him, too, and I don't want him to see it yet. I've just got up, so it'll be around ten-thirty before I get to Deerhaven. OK?"

"We'll look forward to seeing you."

"You can tell Mandy about her present!"

Felicity did, as soon as she got off the phone.

"A present?" Mandy's eyes lit up. "Goody. And my birthday's not even anytime soon!"

But apparently Jordan's was.

"He's going to be thirty-five on Friday," Lacey remarked after she turned up and was unloading gaily wrapped packages onto the kitchen table. "And I got him a present in Accra. I want you to hide it here, give it to him on his birthday if I'm not around. I think I'm going to be home for a week, but I never know what's going to come up. This is for you." She handed a package to Felicity. "And this is for you, Mandy."

"Thank you!" Mandy said, and immediately tore into the pretty paper.

"Lacey, you shouldn't have brought me anything," Felicity protested.

Lacey dismissed her comment with an airy gesture. "It's just a length of silk. I thought you could run yourself up a nice dress."

Meanwhile, Mandy had unwrapped her gift and found it was a red leather purse, decorated with orange beads.

Delightedly, she opened it and when she saw it contained a set of three dainty dolls in saris, her pleasure was complete. Giving her aunt a happy hug, she said, "Thank you so much, Aunt Lacey," before turning to Felicity.

"Hurry up," she said. "Let's see yours, Fizzy."

Felicity's dress-length was of shot silk, in glorious shades of pink and navy and fuchsia.

"Oh, Lacey, it's *gorgeous.*"

"It'll make a fabulous dress," Lacey said. "You'll look stunning in those colors."

"Thank you so much, I can't wait to make it up!"

Mandy sat on a chair and stood her dolls on the table. "What did you get for Daddy?"

"Something special." Lacey's eyes twinkled. "But you'll have to wait for his birthday to find out."

"Are we having a party for him?" Mandy asked.

Lacey said, "What a brilliant idea, Mandy. Let's do that. Felicity?"

"Well…sure, of course. We'd have it here?"

"Mmm. I'll help you if I can. It's too bad Alice is so close to her due date or she could have come over. But never mind, there'll be four of us and it'll be a lot of fun. Do you think you can have your dress ready by then?'' She looked questioningly at Felicity.

"Oh…yes, I'm sure I can.''

"How about you, Mandy? Do you have a pretty dress?''

"I have a scrumptious dress that Daddy bought me. It's yellow with white spots and I haven't worn it once yet!''

"So we're all set.'' Lacey's silver hoop earrings glinted as she flicked back her black hair. "Oh, I just *adore* parties. And maybe it's just as well Alice can't come,'' she added in an aside to Felicity. "Dermid would have had to come, too, and he'd have put a dampener on everything!''

"I met Dermid,'' Felicity said, and explained how it had come about. "I found him charming.''

"He can be,'' Lacey said. "But never to me. Well—'' she grinned mischievously "—you can't win 'em all! Now, let's get the plans for this party under way. And remember, Mandy, not a whisper about it to your father. It has to be kept a secret, so it's a wonderful surprise. It'll be so much fun to see the look on his face. I can hardly wait!''

CHAPTER NINE

NEXT morning, Lacey phoned Felicity to say she was on her way to the airport.

"I have to go to Scotland," she wailed. "To fill in for Kinga Koss, who's come down with chickenpox. The shoot's to be in some Highland glen where there'll be nothing to drink but whiskey, and nobody to speak to but red-haired barbarians in tartan skirts, playing bagpipes and flinging tree trunks at each other!"

Felicity chuckled. "Cabers, Lacey. And kilts. And I'm sure you'll survive. It really is beautiful there, as are the people."

"I know, I'll love it, but I may not get back in time for the party."

"Oh, that would be a huge disappointment!"

"If everything goes smoothly and the weather co-operates, I *could* be home latish Friday afternoon at soonest."

"If you do, will you come here directly from the airport?"

"Yes—oops, have to go. 'Bye for now!"

"'Bye, Lacey."

Felicity put down the phone, and as she turned she saw Jordan standing in the kitchen doorway.

"What's up with Lacey?" he asked.

"She's going to Scotland for a shoot. She's hoping to get home on Friday."

"So...what was that about coming here directly from the airport?"

"She...um...we had plans to get together on Friday evening. If she does get back by then, I suggested she come right here. She could have dinner with us—"

"She'll probably have filled up with lettuce leaves on the flight," he said dryly. "It'll be surprising if she manages more than a sprig of grapes when she gets here. I sometimes worry about her, she's so damned thin."

"She eats well, Jordan, but with her metabolism, she doesn't gain an ounce." Felicity moved to the sink. "Have you heard anything from Alice? She must be getting pretty weary, now that her due date's coming up."

"I talked to Dermid last night. The doc's keeping a close eye on her. And Alice, of course, is being super careful. Things being the way they are with Dermid, they don't want to do anything to jeopardize the pregnancy."

"Is there some problem with Dermid?"

"I thought Lacey might have mentioned it." Jordan took an apple from the fruit basket on the table. "Not too long after Dermid and Alice married, Dermid was diagnosed with cancer. There was a strong possibility that after his chemo sessions, he wouldn't be able to father children so on his doctor's advice, he had some sperm frozen beforehand. Dermid's had a clean bill of health for the past several years and since the ranch is now doing well, they both felt ready to have their first child."

"You mean...they could have another?"

"They have a second fertilized egg stored at a Toronto fertility clinic. Cryogenically frozen. And if all goes well this time around, then in a couple of years, they plan to go ahead and give their son a baby sister.''

"They know the sex already?"

He nodded.

"That's amazing. And I'm so happy for them.''

"They both love kids, and I'm sure they'd have tried to adopt if things hadn't worked out." He shrugged. "That would have been their choice."

"But not yours?"

"Nah, not mine. But hey, to each his own, right?"

His lightly spoken words dropped into Felicity's heart like ice-cold pebbles.

She'd decided, before falling asleep last night, that she would put off telling him about Mandy till the very last minute possible. She'd let him enjoy the surprise party and his one last evening of true happiness. But she'd have to tell him on Saturday morning, and before her mother phoned, because if she didn't, her mother would take it out of her hands.

Dermid phoned at quarter after ten on Thursday evening.

Felicity had planned on having an early night, so after enjoying a cool shower, she had come downstairs in her robe and nightie to let RJ in, when the call came through.

"Is Jordan there?" Dermid asked without preamble.

"Sorry, he isn't. He went back to the office after dinner to meet a client and he's not home yet."

"Could you give him a message when he comes in?" Dermid sounded elated. "I'm over here, in North Vancouver, at Lions Gate Hospital. Alice gave birth to our baby boy just fifteen minutes ago. Jack McTaggart. Eight pounds ten, healthy as a horse. And Mom's terrific, too!"

"Oh, I'm so thrilled! Congratulations, Dermid! But…why aren't you on the island? I understood Alice was to have her baby in Nanaimo."

"She went into labor last night, and things were getting complicated so they sky-lifted her over to Lions Gate. I didn't phone earlier because I wanted to spare Jordan the worry of knowing his sister was in labor till it was safely over. But all's well now, couldn't be better!"

"That's wonderful. Look, I can let you have Jordan's cell phone number if you'd like to talk to him yourself."

"No, that's OK. I want to get back to Alice. Will you tell him?"

"I'll be glad to!"

After she hung up, Felicity stood dreamily for a few moments, sharing the couple's joy, and then she called Jordan to pass the news on to him.

After he'd expressed his relief and delight, he said, "Look, I don't know when I'll get out of here, but I'll stop by the wine store on the way home, pick up a bottle of champagne. We'll celebrate. Will you wait up?"

"Yes," she said. "Of course!"

But she wasn't about to celebrate in her nightie and robe! As soon as she'd put down the phone, she hurried upstairs with RJ scampering at her heels, and changed into a dress. Then after slipping her feet into flat sandals, she left RJ dozing on her bed and popped through to check on Mandy—who was sound asleep in her crib— before going down to the sitting room.

The sun had been beating in all day, and though the patio doors were open, the room was still stiflingly hot. Kicking off her thongs, she curled up in an armchair with a book, intending to read till she heard Jordan come in. But within minutes, she found herself drifting off to sleep.

Some time later she woke with a start, jarred from sleep by the crunch of car tires on gravel.

She brushed down the full skirt of her dress, flicked her braid back over her shoulder, and headed for the kitchen. She'd just got there when the back door opened and Jordan came in.

With his battered old briefcase in one hand, the champagne bottle in a tall brown paper bag in the other, and his suit jacket over his arm, he heeled the door closed.

"Hi," he said. "Thanks for waiting up. Sorry, Felicity, I didn't realize I'd be so late. Offers, counteroffers, you know how it is."

Felicity glanced at her watch and got a shock to see that it was after midnight. "Good heavens, I'd no idea it was this time. But no problem." She relieved him of his jacket. "I dropped off and had a nice sleep!"

She held on to the jacket, savoring the feel of the fine linen, loving the scent of him that clung to it. "You must be exhausted."

"Yeah," he said. "It's been a busy day."

Setting the paper bag upright on the table he heaved the briefcase onto the counter. His sky-blue shirt looked as tired as he did. "I'll pop over to the hospital to visit with Alice tomorrow. Do you want to come? We'll take Mandy to see her new cousin." Yawning, he rolled up his shirtsleeves to just below the elbow, undid his navy silk tie, opened the shirt's top two buttons.

Felicity ached to walk into his arms. Instead she allowed herself the sensuous pleasure of smoothing out his jacket with her fingertips after draping it over the back of a chair. "I don't know Alice, I've never met her. Why don't you and Mandy go, and—"

"Uh-uh. We'll all go. You were bound to meet Alice sooner or later, and this is a good chance to make it sooner. You'll like her, she's one in a million. And she'll like you, too, that goes without saying."

Alice might well like her, but Jordan himself might not even want to set eyes on her again after tomorrow. So why not take advantage of every single opportunity to be with him...while he still wanted to be around her? The voice of her conscience niggled at her. *Don't you think that's being rather selfish?* She ignored it. For once, she was going to be selfish. After Saturday, she doubted she'd ever be happy again.

"Then...yes, I'll come." She watched him fish the champagne bottle out of the tall bag. "Won't you have to chill that?"

"They did at the wine store."

"Oh, good. So...how did things go this evening? Did your clients get the British Properties estate at the price they wanted?"

"Yeah. Finally. And I got the listing for their penthouse condo downtown."

"Ah, a back-to-back!" she teased.

He quirked an amused eyebrow. "The lady's catching on to the lingo!" Yawning again, he slipped the champagne bottle into the fridge. "Can you give me a couple minutes to freshen up? The air conditioning at the office quit around seven, it was hotter than hell down there. I need to have a cold shower, but I'll make it quick."

He swept up his jacket. "I'll be back before you even get the glasses out!" he promised. And added, as he left, "I'll look in on my little princess while I'm upstairs."

His little princess. Every time he talked in that adoring way about Mandy, Felicity felt as if he had squeezed another drop of blood from her heart.

And it also forced her to remember, with painful reluctance, her mother's most recent phone call.

"Felicity, you have to *tell* him! You're not being fair, either to me *or* to Jordan Maxwell. Every single day you put it off, is another day for him to grow to treasure that child more. Do *you* think that's being fair?"

"No, Mom, I don't. But…he's a wonderful man…and a wonderful Dad…and I can't *bear* to hurt him."

Silence at the other end. And then, in a gentler voice, her mother said, "By delaying, you're only going to hurt him more. Felicity, you have till noon Saturday. I won't phone you again until then. But if, by Saturday noon, you haven't told him that Denny is Mandy's father, as sure as I live and breathe I'll come over and tell him myself!"

Felicity had been trembling when she came off the phone.

An ultimatum.

Her mother was a sweet and giving woman, but where her family was concerned, she was a tiger.

Felicity was still lost in her bleak thought when Jordan came back.

"Hey," he said. And added in a tone of mock horror, "Where are the glasses? I give the woman one simple job and—"

"Sorry!" She cleared her thoughts, and focused her attention on him and—

Oh, dear, unlike her, he apparently didn't mind celebrating in his night attire! His robe, dark blue and heavy silk, was belted and barely reached to mid-calf. If anything could have distracted her from worrying about her mother's upcoming deadline, it was the sight of the man she loved standing before her in a robe and…and what?

Was he wearing anything under it?

She swiveled around, her heart pounding, and moved over to the cabinet where the glasses were kept.

She took a moment to steady herself before taking down two crystal flutes, but when she turned around again, Jordan was right behind her—so close she could smell the fresh scent of soap and the minty tang of toothpaste.

"Let's go through to the sitting room." His eyes were as warm as his voice. "Make ourselves comfortable."

"It's still awfully hot in there." She tried to hide her nervousness. "All the rooms facing south are."

"How about your sewing room then?"

It faced north and would certainly be cooler. But it would also be more…intimate, and she'd rather have avoided having him in her private domain. But she could hardly refuse. It was, after all, his house! And he'd had a very hard day; he needed to relax. "Yes, it's better up there."

"Right, let's go!"

Swinging the champagne bottle forward in an "after you" gesture, he stood back to give her access to the corridor, and then followed just behind her.

As they walked up the stairs, he felt a heady rush of excitement as he anticipated what lay ahead.

She could have no idea how much he'd banked on her still being up when he got home, regardless of how late it had been. And when he'd found her in the kitchen, looking like a dream in a pretty violet dress, with her cheeks flushed pink and her gray eyes bright, he'd almost dropped the champagne bottle, she'd so dazzled him.

But he'd managed to keep his cool. He'd managed not to reach out like some Neanderthal and grab her, although everything in him ached to haul her into his arms and kiss her till she was limp with longing.

But that wouldn't do. Felicity Fairfax was as fine and elegant as the crystal flutes she was carrying across the landing. And he would treat her the way she deserved to be treated—with sensitivity and tenderness.

She said, softly, "I'm going to shut Mandy's window."

"OK if I go on into the sewing room?"

"Of course." She handed him the two glasses. "But don't open the champagne till I get there!"

She pushed Mandy's door open and as she slipped into the room, he walked into the sewing room.

One of Mandy's toy boxes lay upside down on the hearth, magazines and storybooks littered the coffee table, and from a chair by the sewing machine a spill of pink, navy and fuchsia silk pooled on the carpet like a Monet painting.

He'd just set the bottle and glasses on the mantelpiece, when Felicity burst into the room.

"Jordan—" she was eager, breathless "—come quick!"

She darted off again, and wondering what was going on, he strode across the room and out to the landing. She was at Mandy's door, waiting for him.

When he reached her, she grabbed the sleeve of his robe. "Ssh," she whispered. "Come and see…"

He followed her into the room, which was dimly lit by the night-light and pleasantly cool. His eyes zeroed in on Mandy's crib, but just as he realized the crib was unoccupied, Felicity pulled his sleeve again.

"No," she whispered. "Here!"

She led him over to the bed, and there was his daughter, curled up and sound asleep, under the light quilt Felicity had made, and which she'd arranged on the bed the morning after she'd finished it.

He did a double take. "She wasn't here when I checked ten minutes ago! I actually walked over to the crib, and ran a hand over her head. She was there all right, and she was out like a light."

"Maybe the sound of the water running disturbed her...or maybe it was your touch on her head. Whatever it was, it woke her...and she—for whatever reason—decided it was time for her to sleep here, in her own little bed."

"Well, I'll be..."

"It's *wonderful,* isn't it?" She looked up at him now, her eyes brilliant with joy.

"Yeah." He put an arm around her shoulders and pulled her to him in a sideways hug. "Wonderful that she's finally made the transition, and on her own. I guess all this time she's been afraid to give up the crib, it was like a security blanket, holding memories of sleeping at your place, where she felt safe. Now she must feel safe here, too. Her mother disappeared out of her life, but now she must feel confident that I'm not about to do the same. She knows she can count on her daddy to be around."

He saw tears well up in Felicity's eyes, and as always, her love for his child filled him with awe. And increased his love for her.

Keeping his arm around her, he eased her out onto

the landing, and pulled the door closed behind them. He was in no hurry to release her—and she seemed in no hurry to be released. Instead, as he pulled her into an embrace, she slipped her arms around him and with a trembling sigh, rested her cheek against his chest.

Her braid had slid over his hand. Heart thudding, he undid the narrow velvet ribbon securing it. She made no protest. And then he undid the pleated hank. Spreading it over her shoulders like a fan of sunlight, he buried his face in it, inhaling the musky peach-scented strands.

She shivered. Then she pressed closer to him, and closer still, as if she couldn't get enough of him.

He tried in vain to keep his arousal in check. "Why," he asked hoarsely, "aren't you fighting me tonight?"

The answer—the one she couldn't give—drummed through Felicity's head:

Because I'm going to break your heart tomorrow.

And it would be "tomorrow" for it was well after midnight and already Friday.

And it was his birthday. She couldn't wish him "Happy Birthday," because she and Lacey and Mandy had agreed to pretend they hadn't remembered it. But tonight she would do everything possible to ensure his happiness…happiness that would be short-lived, for tomorrow he would hate the memory of it. But resolutely she closed her mind to "tomorrow," and to all the other tomorrows to come.

"Why?" he urged again, his breath warm on her lips, his green eyes aflame with passion and dark with need.

"Because I love you, my darling, and I want you to be happy."

With a soft groan, he kissed her again. And again, and again. And then she felt his hand cup her breast, tenderly, sweetly. She sagged against him, while with light fingertips he caressed it and brought it swiftly to a swollen peak. Aching with need, she could only whimper in acquiescence when he swept her up in his arms and carried her to his room.

She herself had changed his bed sheets that morning, had brushed them to flat perfection with the palm of her hands, breathing in the summer-scent of sun-dried linen. But never had she thought that before the day was out, the man she loved so dearly would be laying her on his bed.

Her sandals had fallen to the floor as he carried her, her hair cascaded over the pillow as he set her down.

The sun had set. The room was in shadow, the slatted blinds closed. But still she could see him as he undid the belt of his robe, took off the robe, threw it on a chair, leaving him naked but for a pair of briefs.

All the time, he kept his eyes on her. And as he approached her, those eyes grew smokier. When he lay down beside her, his gaze had become so dark, with intent and with need, a shudder of expectation rippled through her, from the still-tingling nub of her breasts to every raw nerve in her body.

Desire left her limp, and so weak she lay in a state of mindless surrender while he unbuttoned her dress and slipped it off. He let his adoring gaze drift slowly over her body, now barely covered by her bra and bikini panties.

And when he turned her so that they faced each other, their eyes locked in a mist of desire.

"You want this, too?" he asked. But he knew she did; he was already unhooking the front clasp of her bra.

Her throat was so choked she could only nod.

His lips curved in a smile. And then the smile faded as he caressed her again. His features tightened, just as her breasts tightened, too.

She thought she'd never experienced such pleasure, but when he lowered his head and kissed her breast, caressed it with his tongue, she knew she'd been wrong. With unfamiliar sensations quivering inside her, she heard a throaty gasp and realized it was her own.

And then he ran a hand down over her ribs, and farther. He slipped off her panties, and his briefs, and tossed them aside.

No sooner had Felicity heard them rustle on the carpet than he had pulled her over on top of him, her hair spilling down either side of her face, between them, while her body settled over his.

Desire shot through her like a burning arrow.

She moaned, only vaguely aware that he had threaded his hands through her hair and was using it to pull her face down to his.

He kissed her again—sensual lips, teasing tongue, its tantalizing rhythm in perfect harmony with the movements of his hips…a kiss to cherish, a memory to cherish, forever.

When she finally pulled up to draw breath, he tumbled her over and braced himself above her…

She hadn't told him she was a virgin.

The subject had never come up.

But he was going to find out any moment now…

But by the time he did, it was too late to stop.

"You should have told me," he murmured, a long time later.

She loved the way he was holding her close, stroking her hair, sleepily adding a whispered, "My darling."

"Would it have made a difference?" she whispered back, slipping a hand over his, loving its hard-boned strength.

"I'd have gone more slowly, been more gentle..."

Her sigh was soft as the dawn. "I loved it." She snuggled against him, loving everything about him. "Exactly the way it was."

The twitter of sparrows and the *cheer-up, cheer-up* of a perky robin woke Felicity from sleep.

Nestled against Jordan, with one of his arms lying over her, her back touch-to-touch with his chest, she felt his heartbeats thudding steadily against her shoulder. And for a long bittersweet moment, she allowed herself to luxuriate in the exquisite glory of this intimacy, and to remember their wonderful lovemaking of the night before.

Then, holding her breath and with the utmost care, she worked her way out of his embrace, and slipped off the bed.

Retrieving her dress from the carpet, she wrapped it around herself before picking up her undies and sandals.

Then she tiptoed, barefoot, to the door, and crept silently away.

"Fizzy, when are you going to ice Daddy's birthday cake?" Mandy sat at the kitchen table, her spoon poised over her cereal plate as she looked at Felicity.

"I'll do it when he takes you to see your aunt Alice and—" Felicity broke off and put a finger to her lips. "Ssh, I think I hear him coming."

Jordan had slept late, and now, as his steps came closer, she felt her cheeks grow warm. She'd just made a pot of coffee for him, and when he came into the kitchen, she busied herself taking down a mug from the cupboard.

"Hi, princess!" he said.

"Hi, Daddy."

He made a beeline for Felicity and taking the mug from her hand, gave her a tender, lingering kiss that left her weak at the knees.

Holding her away from him, he said, with a teasing twinkle in his eyes, "You walked out on me this morning!"

Shyly she lowered her gaze, fixed it on his sea-green tie. "I was afraid Mandy might waken," she fibbed, "And come through and see...you know." She glanced at the child, but Mandy had become engrossed in studying a green plastic frog that Felicity had found in the cereal packet.

"So?" He tipped her chin up with his fingertips. "What if she had seen us in bed together?"

"She might have...mentioned it...to Lacey...or to Alice, this afternoon—"

"Darling, they're going to know about us soon enough. I plan on making an honest woman of you before too long. But we'll talk later. Right now, I'm going to have a quick coffee and then I must be on my way." His lips twitched. "Morningstar's going to give me hell if I'm late. But, sweetheart—" he gave her a hug "—it was well worth it. Last night was the most wonderful of my life."

Felicity felt guilt gnawing at her heart. Tomorrow, when she told him about Mandy, he was going to remember last night…and wonderful was the last word that would come to his mind. But for now, she had to keep up this charade, although it wasn't going to be easy.

She looked at him as he poured himself a mug of coffee. Did he remember it was his birthday? He'd made not a single mention of it. Perhaps he'd forgotten all about it. But she still had to make sure he'd be here for dinner.

The phone rang, and he answered it.

"Oh, hi, Dermid. How's it going?"

He listened for a while, and then said, "That's great. OK if I come over to see her this afternoon?"

Again he listened, before saying, "Yeah, later on will be fine. You can come back with us. Have dinner. Stay the night. No? OK. Hang on a sec."

He turned to Felicity. "Alice's getting home tomorrow. Is it OK if Dermid comes for dinner this evening? He won't be staying the night, he's putting up at a friend's place."

"Of course."

"Dermid, that's fine. See you at the hospital then."

After he'd put down the phone, he said, "Are you sure it's OK, Felicity? You can cope with an extra one for dinner?"

"Oh, yes. And…you'll eat with us?"

"Yeah, I'll make a point of it."

"Good. If Dermid's going to join us, and possibly Lacey, we should have something special for dinner and I'll need to prepare. I'll skip going to the hospital, though. I'll get everything going while you and Mandy are out."

"Fair enough." He ruffled Mandy's hair. "So it's just you and me, kiddo!"

Mandy sent Felicity a conspiratorial glance before saying, airily, "Just you and me, Dad. That'll give Fizzy time to prepare a *really* special dinner." She giggled; and then put her hands over her mouth.

Jordan lifted one eyebrow. "What's so funny?"

"Nothing, Daddy!" Another giggle escaped. She picked up the green frog and balanced it on the rim of her plate. "It's just this little frog, he's got such a funny old face he makes me laugh every time I look at him!"

Jordan grinned and looked at Felicity. "This kid of mine," he said. "Isn't she something? I don't know what I'd ever do without her!"

Mandy beamed up at him. "You won't ever have to, Daddy! I'm not going anywhere…and that's a promise!"

CHAPTER TEN

ON ARRIVAL at the office, Jordan checked his watch.

And rolled his eyes.

Morningstar was going to be on the warpath, even though it was the first time since Felicity had moved in that he'd been late for the morning meeting.

"Hi, Bette!" he called out as he loped toward the reception desk. "How's it going? Get that raise yet?"

"Today was not the time to ask! Phil's in one sour mood. He's been out here three times since the meeting started, asking if you hadn't turned up yet." Her expression became evasive. "I'm sorry, Jordan..."

"Sorry? About what?"

She lowered her gaze, fiddled about with some papers. "He did warn you...when he gave you that extra week to get your personal life in order...it was your last chance..."

Morningstar was going to fire him?

Oh, this was just great. On his birthday, too—although not a soul had remembered it. He couldn't have expected Felicity to, she wouldn't even know it was today. But Bette had always given him a birthday hug. His sisters had always sent a gift. Today, nothing. Nada. Zilch.

And now...Morningstar was going to fire him.

"Thanks," he said, "for giving me the heads-up."

As he strode grimly along the corridor, he heard the sound of voices coming from the boardroom. The moment he entered, conversation stopped. All eyes turned to him. Tension sizzled in the air. A sense of…waiting.

"You're late!" Morningstar's harsh-angled face gave nothing away. "What the devil kept you? No, don't tell me, I don't want to know. Sit down! I've got something to say to you."

"I prefer," Jordan said, "to stand." To face the firing squad upright. He challenged Morningstar with his eyes. Go ahead, buster. Get it over with.

His boss shoved back his chair and lumbered to his feet. "OK, here's the picture. It pains me to say it, but this office is going to be losing one of its best men…"

"Go on." Jordan didn't flinch.

Morningstar paused, milking the moment. And then, with a twinkle in his eye, he said, "I've decided to retire."

Jordan gawked at him, before sending a startled gaze around the table. Jack LaRoque winked, the others grinned.

"At least," Morningstar continued, "the *doc* has decided that I'm to retire. Heart, stress, ulcers, you name it, I've got it. So…I'm stepping down at the end of the month, and I need a manager. Since today's your birthday, Maxwell, I thought I'd offer you the job."

Right on cue, Bette came into the boardroom carrying an iced cake adorned with a mass of flickering candles.

Setting it on the table with a "Ta da!" and a flourish, she handed Jordan a knife, while he stood, dizzy with surprise, and a slow dawning of pleasure, as his colleagues congratulated him on his promotion, and wished him many happy returns of his birthday.

"There you are," Bette said. "Cut that, while I bring through a fresh pot of coffee. And by the way, since you're going to be the new boss...how about that pay raise!''

Morningstar's hatchety face was, for once, creased in a smile. ''She's started in on you already, has she? Good luck, Maxwell.'' He slapped Jordan heartily on the back. ''You're going to need it.''

As soon as he politely could, Jordan found a quiet corner of the boardroom and took out his cell phone. He needed to call Felicity. He needed to tell her his news.

But he wouldn't mention the birthday celebration. After all, turning thirty-five wasn't that big a deal, was it? He would let the day slip by, unnoticed.

''Hi,'' he said as she answered the phone. ''Guess what? You're talking to the new manager of Morningstar Realty!''

A stunned silence. Then, ''Oh, Jordan, how lovely! I'm so *happy* for you! And we'll be able to celebrate tonight at dinner—''

Morningstar was calling on him to make a speech.

''Felicity, I have to go. Give Mandy a kiss from her daddy, tell her I'll be home around four, and we'll go see the baby. 'Bye, darling. Love you...can't wait to see you.''

As he hung up the phone Jordan realized that he felt as close to Felicity as if she were already his wife. Felt it in a way he never had with Marla.

He'd found out, right after he and Marla married, that she wasn't the soul mate she'd seemed to be. As soon as that gold wedding band was safely on her finger, she revealed herself in her true colors. And those colors weren't pretty. She'd been utterly self-centered, never in the least interested in what he was doing...except if it related to money.

What had finally killed his love for her was when she became pregnant and said she'd have the baby only if he agreed to her farming it out to a sitter. He'd desperately wanted the child, so he'd had no choice in the matter. She'd loved no one, but herself. And maybe Denny Fairfax, although he doubted that she'd cared much for him, other than that he showed her a good time.

Felicity loved him for himself, not for what he could give her...although he'd have given her the world if he could.

A glow warmed his heart as he walked up to the head of the table to say a few words. He would take Felicity out on the weekend; together they would choose her engagement ring.

And he would be the happiest man on earth.

"Daddy's home!" Excitement trilled in Mandy's voice as she called from the back door stoop into the kitchen. "Hide the party hats, Fizzy!"

Felicity stowed the hats in a drawer, and swept up the scraps left over from the colored paper she and Mandy had used to make them. She just had time to toss them into the garbage, when she heard Jordan say, "So...how's my best girl tonight?"

"Daddy, you have *two* best girls, me and *Fizzy!*"

Felicity heard him chuckle. "Yup," he drawled, "You're right about that!" and then he appeared in the doorway with a grinning Mandy carried piggyback, her sun-browned arms around his strong neck in a stranglehold.

He gave Felicity a bone-melting smile as he dumped his old briefcase on the counter and crossed to where she was standing. When he kissed her, he tasted of summer and he smelled so warm and sexy her knees sagged.

"When," Mandy demanded, "are we going to the hospital?"

Jordan gave Felicity one last kiss—but the look in his eyes promised more—before sliding Mandy down to the floor. "Have you heard from Lacey?" he asked.

Felicity shook her head. "But she could still turn up in time for dinner. Let's hope so."

"You do know that she and Dermid don't exactly hit it off? It might be a more peaceful meal," he added with a lopsided smile, "if she *weren't* to turn up!"

"Daddy!" Mandy grabbed his hand—or as much of it as her little fingers allowed. "Let's go!"

He looked down at her amusedly. "You can't wait to see that new cousin of yours, can you! Just give me a couple of minutes to freshen up and then we'll hit the road!"

Felicity was hanging up a Happy Birthday streamer in the dining room when she heard a car door slamming. After quickly finishing her task, she went to look out the window, and saw a Sunshine cab drawing away.

She went out into the foyer and was just in time to see the front door opening and Jordan's sister sweep in.

"Hi, Lacey! Oh, I'm so glad you've made it!"

Swinging the door shut behind her, Lacey tossed down her travel case and the roomy leather bag which held her makeup and modeling accoutrements.

"Fizzy!" she called gaily. "It's great to see you!" She whirled over to Felicity and gave her a tight hug. "Where's everybody?" she asked eagerly. "Jordan still at work? Where's my darling niece? Oh, I'd give anything for a glass of chilled wine...is the sun over the yardarm yet? I slept on the plane, slept through every- thing, the drinks, the meal, the movie..." Her sleek black hair flew out around her shoulders as she spun around to face the stairs. "Mandy?" she called up. "Honey? Your aunt Lacey's here!"

Felicity laughed. "If you'd slow down for just a sec- ond...where on earth do you get all that energy from? Doesn't your body know the meaning of jet lag? I've lots to tell you. Come through to the kitchen and I'll fill you in on everything that's happened."

As Lacey tucked her arm into Felicity's, Felicity led the way to the kitchen.

"Mandy's not here." She took a bottle of dry Riesling from the fridge, and held it up. "This OK?"

"Fab!"

Felicity took two wineglasses out, and uncorking the wine, went on, "She's with Jordan, at Lions Gate Hospital."

"Hospital? Oh, dear, what's—"

"Nothing's wrong!" Felicity poured the wine, handed Lacey a glass. "Alice had her baby last night and..."

Amid constant interruptions from an excited Lacey who wanted to know every last detail, Felicity told her the whole story, and finished by saying, "Jordan and Mandy should be home any minute...and Dermid. He's coming for dinner."

"Oh, he is, is he! Just wait, he'll take every chance he can to put me down!"

"Surely not."

"Oh, he'll be very subtle about it, but he never fails to hold Alice up as the perfect example of what a woman *should* be—barefoot, pregnant, and rooted in the kitchen—certainly not prancing around the world, skinny as a rail and making oodles of money for 'swanning around doing nothing' as he puts it! There's something about Scotsmen,'' she said with an elegant sniff, "that makes me wonder if they'll ever notice we're no longer in the tenth century!''

Felicity was not about to get into a discussion of Dermid or any other Scotsman! "Let's go out to the patio, it's baking hot in here with the oven on but you did suggest I make lasagna since it's Jordan's favorite dinner.''

"Mmm, and it smells just yummy! But isn't there something I can do to help? Wash some lettuce…or…?'' Gracefully, the model waved her glass in the air.

Felicity laughed. She knew from what Lacey had told her that she rarely cooked, scarcely knew how to boil an egg. "Everything's under control. But thanks anyway.''

"If you're sure…''

But Lacey was already aiming for the corridor!

"I can't wait to see Alice!'' she announced as they walked across the lounge and out onto the patio. "And baby Jack! If we weren't having this party tonight I'd scoot over and visit…but I'll go first thing tomorrow.''

She ensconced herself in one of the cushioned loungers and stretched out languidly. "Now, Felicity, tell me what *you've* been up to all week!'' She took a long sip from her glass, and after murmuring appreciatively, asked, "Did you have time to make up that silk?''

"Yes, I did. I'm so pleased with the dress, it's the prettiest one I've ever had.''

"Good! And what else?''

"Um…oh, Mandy has finally given up sleeping in her crib. Jordan and I are *so* relieved."

"Fabulous! Poor kid, she's had a tough time of it, but she must really feel settled and secure now at Deerhaven. You've done a great job, Felicity. And not only with Mandy, with my brother, too. I've never seen Jordan as happy as he is these days."

Yes, Jordan was happy. But Felicity knew she herself had never been more unhappy. If only things had been different. But from tomorrow on, Jordan would be lost to her.

And along with that loss would probably be the loss of Lacey's friendship, which she had come to value. More than anything in the world she yearned to be a permanent part of Jordan's family, but that was going to be impossible.

They chatted for a while, until Lacey suddenly said, "They're here!"

Felicity listened, and heard the crunch of car tires on the graveled forecourt.

Lacey rose in one fluid movement, all long arms and longer legs. "I'm going to grab my things and go upstairs before they come in." Glancing down wryly at her travel-weary outfit, she added, "I wouldn't want the laird to see me looking less than perfect, he might just get the idea that I'm human after all! If you don't mind, I'll use your bathroom—I'll have a quick shower now and you can have yours when you come up. Don't be long. We'll get dressed together. It'll be fun, like being teenagers again!"

Yes, it would be just like that, Felicity thought sadly. And she'd better make the most of it, as this would be the one and only time it was likely to happen.

*   *   *

"Jack's so *small*, Aunt Lacey!" Mandy hopped about impatiently as Felicity brushed her hair. "And his face is all red and wrinkled, but he's really cute!"

"I bet he is, and I can't wait to see him tomorrow." Seated at the dresser, Lacey smoothed a hand over her immaculate topknot, before leaning forward to adjust the lustrous string of pearls glowing at her throat. "There," she said, sitting back, satisfied. "I'm ready."

"We're all ready!" Mandy said as Felicity put down the hairbrush. "Let's go stand and look at ourselves in the mirror!"

Throwing each other amused glances, Felicity and Lacey lined up with her in front of the mirrored closet doors.

"Your dress is stunning," Lacey said to Felicity. "And your hair's fabulous—I've never seen it loose before."

"It looks like falling-down gold," Mandy said.

Lacey laughed delightedly. "You're right, sweetie, that's exactly what it looks like. And your lovely curls are as shiny as gold coins! What a pretty party dress Daddy bought you...same color as your hair!"

"Your dress is pretty, too," Mandy said.

"You're lucky you suit black," Felicity added. "But then, you're so gorgeous, you look good in anything!"

Lacey wrinkled her perfect nose. "My feet aren't gorgeous. I do envy you yours, Felicity, they're so slender and dainty, and they look super in those strappy sandals."

"What's wrong with your feet?" Mandy asked.

"They're so big...the bane of my life!" She regarded her long narrow feet with disdain, although Felicity thought they were very elegant.

Mandy stuck out one of her yellow sandals. "What about *my* feet, Aunt Lacey? Are they dainty, too?"

"The daintiest I've ever seen, darling! And now—" Lacey twirled from the mirror, her eyes sparkling "—let's go find your daddy and uncle Dermid. It's party time!"

Felicity felt a wave of depression sweep over her as they went down the stairs. Jordan had been in such high spirits when he'd come back from the hospital; it was going to be unbearably painful, tomorrow, to shatter his dreams and break his heart.

Her eyes teared up at the prospect, and blinking hard, she said, "You two go ahead, I've forgotten something…"

She ran back upstairs to her bedroom and hurried into the en suite bathroom for a tissue. After dabbing her tears away, she'd just dropped the tissue into the garbage basket, when she remembered she hadn't warned Lacey and Mandy not to let Jordan go into the dining room yet.

She dashed out of the bathroom and across the bedroom and out into the corridor—

And ran headlong into Jordan.

"Oops!" He caught her and then held her away from him, his eyes warm. He'd showered and changed, and smelled of some spicy aftershave. And he was wearing a dark blazer with a white T-shirt and neatly pressed jeans, and he looked so handsome she wanted to weep.

"Hey," he teased, "If I'd known you were so desperate for a hug I'd have given you one when I came home, but you took off so quickly with Mandy you didn't give me a chance."

Then his lips were on hers and after stiffening for a fraction of a second, well aware that she should hold him at bay, she surrendered and slid her arms around his neck.

He held her close and deepened his kiss.

Melting with love for him, she gave herself up completely to sensation. She didn't protest when he walked her back into her room, nor when he ran his hands down her back, nor even when he cupped her bottom and pulled her so intimately to him she knew how much he wanted her.

It intoxicated her. And lost in love and longing, she allowed him to slide a hand up over her hip, up further, over her ribs, to rest for a breathless moment over her heart before he captured her breast. Gently, as she yielded utterly to him, he caressed her till pleasure peaked in the swollen flesh, shooting quivers of desire to every erotic nerve ending in her body and finally coiling in a moist and private place that lay deep within her feminine core.

With a soft sound of arousal in her throat, she arched against him, shamelessly, wantonly. Seductively.

He groaned. His cheek was hot against hers, as was his urgent, "Oh, God, Felicity, I *want* you." He buried his face in the golden cascade of her hair. "I want you so badly it's sheer torture. But the timing's all to hell, my darling, and if we don't stop this right now I'm going to—"

"Daddy?" Mandy's querulous voice, impatient, demanding, floated up the stairwell. "Are you coming?"

With a frustrated mutter, Jordan slid his hand from Felicity's breast, and rested it on her hip. Leaning his brow against hers, he stayed that way for a very long moment, and she sensed he was taking control of himself. And then, he lifted his head and she saw that his green eyes were alight with wry merriment. Taking her hand in his, he led her out to the landing.

Mandy was standing at the foot of the stairs, her face upturned. "Did you hear me shouting, Daddy? I wanted to know if you were coming!"

"Yeah," he said, "I heard you." Straight-faced but giving Felicity's hand a squeeze, he added lightly, "And I was just about to come when you called!"

The surprise party was a huge success.

Jordan had truly believed everyone had forgotten it was his birthday, and he was genuinely delighted with his presents. Dermid had given him an alpaca sweater, made with wool from their own llamas and the garment knitted by Alice herself. Lacey had given him a very grand leather briefcase which she'd bought in India—to "replace that battered antique you've been carting around for years!" And Mandy proudly presented him with a studio portrait of herself and "Fizzy," which, Mandy told Jordan, had been her very own idea but the portrait was the present from them both.

"Fizzy didn't want to be in it," Mandy told Jordan later, when he went up to give her a good-night kiss after Felicity had come downstairs after tucking her in. "She said you wouldn't want a picture of her. But I *made* her be in it, 'cos I said if she didn't then I wouldn't come to the party. Did you want her to be in it, Daddy?"

"Would I want a photo of one of my best girls, or of both my best girls?" he teased her.

"Both," she said, contentedly. "I knew I was right."

After leaving the bedroom, he went back downstairs and met Dermid in the foyer.

"I'm going to leave now," his brother-in-law said

over a yawn. "I didn't get much sleep last night. You don't mind, do you?"

"Of course not."

Dermid hesitated, his expression suddenly very serious. "Felicity's a topper," he said quietly. "Don't let her get away, Jordan."

Jordan clapped a hand on his brother-in-law's shoulder. "Don't worry," he said with a grin. "I don't intend to."

"So, Felicity, did you see it? Did you see the way that man needled me? All through dinner! Honestly, I love my sister dearly, but I sometimes wonder what she sees in—"

"What who sees in…?" Jordan said as he strolled into the room. "Have I missed something?"

Sadness swamped Felicity as she looked at him. This evening had been the most difficult in her life. She'd had to act as though she was enjoying herself, while all the time she'd been torn in two—one half of her yearning desperately to be in Jordan's arms, the other half wallowing in a gut-wrenching dread of what she had to do tomorrow.

Jordan himself had never seemed happier. Every time their eyes had met, his had openly revealed his love for her. Every opportunity he got, he touched her—a hand on her shoulder after he seated her at the dinner table; an arm around her as he walked her to the sitting room; a casual toying with her hair as he sat beside her on the love seat.

It had been agony.

She had never dreamed she could love someone so much. And she had no idea how she was going to live the rest of her life without him.

Lacey was talking. Felicity tried to pay attention.

"…and you would think," Lacey sputtered, "that just because *Alice* is an earth-mother type, every other woman—and yours truly in particular!—should love having babies, too, should love to stay home and grow plump and should treat the men in their lives as gods! I *tell* you, Jordan—"

Jordan's laugh rolled out. "Dermid's only teasing you, Lace. And if you didn't get so uppity when he takes the mickey—"

"And why wouldn't I get uppity? He thinks being a model is the most useless job on the face of the earth and he also thinks I don't have a single brain in my head."

"You know damn well why he thinks that—you always put on that dumb act when he's around. Like tonight, when he talked about the possibility of cloning alpacas and then mentioned Dolly, you put on that wide-eyed look and said, 'You mean they've managed to clone Dolly Parton? How could I have missed that? It *must* have been in *all* the tabloids!'"

Lacey's cheeks dimpled in a mischievous smile. "Did you see his face? I thought he was going to have a conniption."

Felicity let the conversation wash around her. She had developed a pounding headache; it felt as if something in her right temple was about to burst. She pressed her fingertips against it, to try to get relief.

"Felicity?" Jordan's voice had an edge of concern. "Are you all right?"

"Oh…I'm fine…really. Just a little tired."

Lacey jumped to her feet. "No wonder, you've had such a busy day. That was a terrific meal, and it's been a super evening, but you must be ready for bed." She turned to Jordan. "Should I call a cab, or will you drive me?"

"I'll drive."

"Thanks. Give me a couple of minutes—" she made for the door "—while I go up and grab my things."

As Lacey ran upstairs, Felicity said to Jordan, "I'm sorry to break up the party."

"It was time. I'm just sorry you're feeling so tired." He'd taken his jacket off after dinner, and now when he put his strong arms around her, she could smell the musky male scent of his body, and feel the contours of his muscled chest against her breast. "You go to bed, and have a good night's sleep."

"I should really finish up in the kitchen—"

"Uh-uh. I'll do that, when I get back."

He kissed her then, his lips as soft as his chest was hard, a kiss that tasted of wine and the chocolate-coated mints Dermid had brought for after dinner. A kiss that she knew she would remember all her life, as it would be the last they would ever share.

"I was hoping," he murmured as Lacey's returning steps sounded on the stairs, "that when we were alone we could continue where we left off earlier...but it can wait, my darling. Until tomorrow!"

Tomorrow.

As his car drew away a few moments later, Felicity stood at the front door watching; and she remained there listening till the sound of its engine faded away into the starry night.

Jordan was so looking forward to tomorrow.

Little did he know the sorrow it was going to bring.

CHAPTER ELEVEN

JORDAN had just got dressed next morning when he heard a scratching sound in the corridor.

On investigation, he discovered RJ was the culprit. The cat had been clawing the door, and when he saw Jordan, he mewed "I need to go out!" before padding off toward the stairs.

Darn cat! But Jordan smiled as he ambled after it. Over the past several weeks, he'd got used to the animal, and realized that he no longer thought of it as a nuisance. Must be lonely for the poor devil, he mused. Maybe one of these days he should get a pal for him.

Felicity's bedroom door was still closed, but as he reached Mandy's, his daughter emerged, her eyes drowsy.

"RJ woke me," she mumbled when she saw Jordan. "I was going to let him out."

"I will," he said. "Do you want to go back to bed?"

"Uh-uh. I'm hungry."

He took her hand and they went down to the kitchen, where RJ was already arched up against the outside door, trying with his right paw to reach up to the doorknob.

Mandy opened the door for him, then she sat up at the table while Jordan set out her cereal and milk.

"Would you like a boiled egg?" he asked.

"Aren't you in a hurry to get to the office?"

"Not this morning. Your aunt Alice and the baby are going home today and your uncle asked if I'd pick them all up and drive them to Horseshoe Bay to catch the ferry.''

''Can I come?''

''No, sweetie. Aunt Alice will be very tired and she'll be busy looking after Jack. You'll stay here with Fizzy and I'll be back before you know it. So, how about a boiled egg and some hot buttered toast?''

''OK, Daddy. Thank you.''

He put her egg on to boil, plugged in the coffeemaker, brewed a pot of raspberry tea for the love of his life! Whistling cheerfully, he slotted whole-wheat bread in the toaster and had just flicked it on, when he heard Mandy say,

''Good morning, Fizzy.''

He turned and saw Felicity had come into the room. Her hair was loose, and in a pink sundress and sandals she looked as glorious as the summer morning.

After giving Mandy a hug, she greeted him with a quiet, ''Good morning, Jordan.''

''Good morning, darling!'' He strode over to her and swept her into his arms. ''I was going to bring you breakfast in bed.'' He claimed her lips in a lingering kiss. ''You should have stayed in bed,'' he murmured against her cheek, which was petal-smooth and fragrant as a dewy rose. ''It would've given me great pleasure to come to your room and—''

''Daddy,'' Mandy said, in a tone of great interest. ''Why are you kissing Fizzy? Are you in *love* with her?''

He put an arm around Felicity's shoulders as he switched his attention to Mandy, who had swiveled around in her seat to look at them. ''Yes, you little spy, I am.''

"Well, she loves you, too. I know that 'cos her eyes go soft when she looks at you."

"Yes, my poppet, I do believe you're right."

"Then—" Mandy regarded him knowingly "—you have to get married. That's what people do, when they're in love. And then," she added, "Fizzy will get to be my mother."

"You'd like that?" he asked.

"I'd like it more than anything."

"Then, my sweet princess, you shall have it because as surely as the sun rises every morning, your precious Fizzy and I are going to be married."

"Promise, Daddy?"

Felicity said, "Jordan—"

"Half a sec, Felicity—"

"Jordan, I need to—"

"Hang on, sweetheart—let me just finish this little conversation with my daughter. Yes, Mandy, I promise. We're going to get married very soon, and you'll be our flowergirl, and just like in your favorite fairy tales, we're all going to live happily ever after."

"Goody!" Mandy wriggled in her chair. "You've promised so now it's gonna happen for *sure!* I can hardly wait—oops, Daddy, time to get the toast before it burns!"

He shot the switch up and caught it before it did. As he buttered it, he noticed Felicity hovering restlessly.

He crossed over to her once he'd attended to Mandy. "So what were you going to say back there, my darling?"

"I need to talk to you. Alone."

"Is there a problem?"

"I don't want to talk—" she lowered her voice "—where Mandy can hear us."

"What's it about?"

"I'll tell you when we're on our own." The words came out on a tremor.

He put a gentle hand on her arm. "Honey—"

She flicked his hand away.

He flinched as if she'd struck him.

Then agitatedly, she gasped, "Oh, I'm *sorry!*"

What the hell was going on? He scrutinized her face, and now on close inspection he could see dark shadows under her eyes and darker shadows in the eyes themselves.

"Sweetheart," he murmured, "*I'*m sorry. Whatever it is, I can see it's important to you. Look, I have to go to the hospital shortly, pick up the McTaggarts and drive them to the ferry. So how about we talk when I get back?"

"This can't wait."

"Not even till—"

"No." Her voice had a hint of desperation. "It can't."

Now he was *really* worried. "In that case, will you give me a minute? Take my coffee and your tea out to the patio and we'll talk there."

When he'd gone, Felicity slumped against the counter. She *had* to tell him before he went out. If he were delayed in getting back, on his return her mother might get to him first and there was no guarantee Adelaide would break the news gently.

Felicity sighed. She'd tried to stop Jordan from promising Mandy there would be a wedding. Promises should never be broken; especially promises to children. But he'd barreled right on, the promise had been made...and Felicity had no doubt that when she'd told him the truth about Mandy, he'd fall over himself in his hurry to retract it.

Mandy pushed back her chair. "Fizzy, I'm finished. May I be excused? I want to watch TV"

"Yes, of course." Felicity felt a pang of utter despair as she looked at Mandy. This dear little girl, with her eyes so trusting, was perhaps never going to be as happy and innocent again as she was at this very moment. With all her heart, Felicity wished she could protect her from the rejection that surely lay ahead; but the chain of events had been set into play a long time ago, and there was nothing she could do now to stop them from unfolding.

Jordan stepped out onto the patio, closed the screen door behind him. "Sorry I was a bit longer than I expected. Where's Mandy?"

"In the den." Felicity watched him sit down across from her at the patio table, watched the warm breeze lift his hair as he reached for his mug. "I hope your coffee's still hot enough for you."

He took a sip. "It's fine." Leaning back in his seat, he put his face up to the sun and said, "What a beautiful morning. Nice for Alice, for the journey home."

Felicity opened her mouth to speak, but when she saw him close his eyes and savor the warmth of the sunshine, she closed it again. Let him at least enjoy these last moments of true peace, before she dropped her bombshell.

She drank her tea, and after finishing it, set the mug

on the table. The clink of china against metal had Jordan opening his eyes. He smiled.

"Soon," he said, "I'll open my eyes every morning and see you right there beside me. Have you thought about a wedding date yet? Let's get married before the snow flies. How about late September? Would that give you enough time to—"

She rose abruptly from her chair. She had to speak now—speak the words that would extinguish the love in his eyes and the joy in his heart. Dread knotted her stomach as she said, "Jordan..." Then suddenly dizzy, she grasped the back of her chair for support.

Jordan got up quickly. "Sweetheart, are you all right?"

She put up a hand to stop him as he started towards her. "Don't. Stay where you are." She sensed his surprise, and his puzzlement, but he stopped.

"Felicity, what the devil's going on?"

"Just...let me—" She drew in a shaky breath. "There is something wrong. What I have to tell you...it's going to upset you...terribly. It's...about Denny. And...your wife."

His expression relaxed. "Sweetheart, we don't need to go into that again. I promise you, I've put it all behind me, it's in the past—"

"No," Felicity said. "It's not."

Frowning, he stuck his hands into the pockets of his chinos. "How can it not be? Denny and Marla...they're both dead."

Felicity cleared her throat. "Jordan, we...that is, my family...and you...we all assumed...or at least somehow got the impression...that Denny and Marla didn't start their affair till last Christmas..."

"That's right. They met at a charity 'do'—"

"No. Oh, they may well have met at a charity 'do,' but it wasn't the one last Christmas. They'd actually met long before that, and their affair had been going on, in secret, for…close to five years."

She could see she'd shocked him. He stared at her for a long moment…and then his eyes narrowed, his gaze became unfocused, as if he were looking back, into the past, trying to remember how it had been. Finally, more to himself than to Felicity, he muttered, "How could I not have seen?"

He jerked his attention back to her and his expression had become guarded. "You must have known I wouldn't relish hearing that my wife had made a fool of me over an even longer period than I'd realized. What good is it going to do, telling me now?"

"There's more, Jordan. I haven't come to the…the most hurtful part yet."

"You think there's something more hurtful than having a wife who had a long-time lover right under my very nose? Good God, Felicity, I'd have given you credit for more sensitivity, considering—"

"Jordan, it's…not only about Denny and Marla, it's about Mandy."

"Keep my daughter out of this!" Anger colored his face. "Don't even talk about her in the same breath as you talk about your brother. You've said enough, Felicity. I don't want to hear any more!"

Features taut, eyes dark with distaste, he spun around and headed toward the patio doors.

Felicity's heartbeats lurched. If she didn't talk quickly, it was going to be too late. He was going to storm away and lord knew when he'd return. She'd hoped to break this more gently to him than her mother would...

But she had run out of time.

"Jordan, wait!"

He ignored her. He reached out to open the screen door.

"Jordan you have to listen!" She saw his fingers curve around the edge of the door. "You see....Mandy isn't your daughter." Her voice had become high, tinged with hysteria. "She's Denny's child."

He froze. As if turned to ice. She'd never seen it happen to anyone before. The sight chilled her to the bone.

But his thoughts wouldn't be frozen. They would be running amok. She couldn't *begin* to imagine what he was thinking...although he probably felt as if the world had tilted and thrown him off the face of the earth.

When at last he turned, his eyes whipped her.

"You're lying." His raspy voice grated her nerves. "What kind of a *vicious* mind could come up with such a—"

"I have proof. Denny left papers." Her tone was low now, and pleading. "For my mother. Mom gave them to me, on the day of his funeral. All the facts are there, all the dates—"

"To *hell* with the dates! Mandy's—"

"And the DNA results...from tests carried out just days after Mandy's birth." Hating what she was doing, she drew the DNA papers from the pocket of her sundress, and held them shakily out to him. "The proof is incontrovertible."

For a moment she thought he wasn't going to move, and then he strode over and snatched the papers from her.

As he scanned them, the sun shone on his head, making each dark strand of hair glisten. She ached to pull his head to her breast, to give him comfort. But she was the last person in the world he'd look to for solace.

He clenched the papers in his fist. With the haunted expression of an innocent man condemned to death, he demanded, in a voice thick with pain, "Why tell me *now?*"

She swallowed hard before answering. "Because...my mother wants Mandy."

He looked at her as if he didn't know who she was. And surely, Felicity thought in anguish, that is how he must feel: she was a stranger to him, just as Denny had once been, walking into his life and destroying it.

"Oh, Jordan, I'm so—"

But he'd whirled away from her again and was opening the screen door. He slammed it to the side with such force she winced. As she ran after him, she saw him stride across the foyer and make for the front door.

"Jordan, please wait—"

He wrenched the door open and charged outside. And before she'd crossed the foyer, she heard his car roar to life.

Hurrying out to the step, she saw him take off down the drive, faster than she'd ever seen him drive before.

"Fizzy?" Mandy materialized beside her. "Has Daddy gone to the hospital?"

Felicity swallowed to relieve the tightness in her throat, before answering. "Yes, that's where he's gone."

But as she and Mandy went inside again, she found herself praying that he had, indeed, gone to the hospital.

She did not even want to think of the alternative.

*   *   *

Adelaide Fairfax phoned Deerhaven at twelve noon.

Felicity had been pacing the kitchen, almost out of her mind with worry about Jordan. Even allowing for the traffic, shouldn't he have been back from the ferry by now? At least she knew he'd gone to the hospital, otherwise Dermid would have called to ask what was keeping him.

Now, when the phone rang, Felicity prayed it would be Jordan. But it was her mother.

"Have you told him?" Adelaide asked without preamble.

"Yes, Mom. I told him."

"So...what did the poor man say?"

Felicity glanced at Mandy who was sitting coloring at the table. "We didn't talk, Mom. He had to go out."

"But he must have said something? When am I going to see Denny's daughter again, Fliss? Did he say when?"

Wearily, Felicity said, "Mom, he didn't say anything. As you can imagine, he was very shocked. It'll take him some time for this to sink in, I can't begin to imagine how he must be feeling right now."

Her mother hesitated, and then said, "He's not the kind of man to do anything...foolish, is he?"

All morning, Felicity had been asking herself the same thing. And her stomach was painfully knotted because of it. "I don't know, Mom. I really don't know."

In a softer voice, her mother said, "I won't call again, dear. I'll wait for you to let me know what's going on. But just remember, Mandy's Denny's daughter, not Jordan Maxwell's, and she should be with us, with her *real* family, because that's where she belongs."

*   *   *

Felicity prowled around the house for the next few hours, hoping that if Jordan didn't turn up, at least he'd phone.

He didn't.

By the time four o'clock rolled around she was going out of her mind with worry. Pacing the sitting room while Mandy rolled a ball across the carpet for RJ, she asked herself what should she do. Should she wait at Deerhaven till Jordan came back? But perhaps he was staying away on purpose, so she and Mandy could be packed and gone before he returned. Or had he, in his tormented state, done something foolish, as Adelaide had suggested he might? She prayed not!

"Fizzy, can we go and play ball out in the garden?"

A watched pot never boils, Felicity reflected wearily, and maybe, in the same way, a watched phone never rings.

"Yes," she said, "let's go outside."

So they trooped out into the sunny afternoon, Mandy with her ball and RJ pitter-pattering along in the rear.

Mandy ran onto the lawn and rolled the ball across the grass. RJ leaped after it. Mandy chortled as he pounced on it, lost his balance, and fell over onto his back.

Felicity stayed close to the house, so she would be sure to hear the phone if it rang.

Jordan stood on the ferry deck, staring down into the swirling water, his thoughts deeper than the ocean below.

When he'd awakened that morning he'd been the happiest man in the world. A scant hour later, that world had been overturned, his emotions sent careening out of control and spiraling down into a desperate kind of hell.

And in that hell had blazed his burning anger at Denny Fairfax and at Marla. Their deception had been vile, their ongoing affair in the face of that deception beyond words—at least any words in *his* vocabulary.

But he'd had to keep his feelings hidden when he'd picked up the McTaggarts as he hadn't wanted to upset Alice, who looked pale and tired. And when he'd driven the family to Horseshoe Bay, it had been obvious that his sister was in no fit state to be dropped off as a foot passenger, so he'd decided to make the crossing with them and drive them home.

Once at the ranch, he'd stopped only long enough to grab a sandwich, but on returning to Departure Bay he'd found a long lineup of vehicles and a one-sailing wait.

Now, at last, he was finally approaching Horseshoe Bay.

He hadn't meant to be away this long. And he felt emotions churning around inside him as he anticipated the scene that lay ahead, once he reached Deerhaven.

"Fizzy, RJ's up in the apple tree, and he's stuck!"

Felicity had been watering potted plants on the patio. Now she put the watering can down and crossed the lawn. Mandy was standing under the gnarled old tree, looking up into the green leafy branches.

"Where is he?" Felicity asked.

"On that branch."

Felicity followed Mandy's pointing finger and spotted the cat. He mewed down at her. *Help me.*

"Can you rescue him?" Mandy's eyes were dark with anxiety. "He must be so scared up there!"

Felicity regarded the tree. "Well, if I got a ladder…"

"Daddy keeps them in the garage."

"Mmm. All right. You stay here, keep an eye on RJ."

Dragging a ladder from the garage, Felicity carted it into the garden and across the lawn. She'd just propped it against the apple tree when she heard the phone ringing.

Her heart leaped. Would it be Jordan?

She ran toward the house, calling back over shoulder, "Keep an eye on RJ, sweetie…and don't go near the ladder!"

Please, she prayed, let it be Jordan who was calling.

It was Joanne.

She'd been away on vacation, and she wanted to chat.

Felicity said breathlessly, "Jo, this is a really bad time. I can't go into it right now but…I'm waiting for a phone call."

"What's happened? You sound *awful!*"

"I can't really talk just now. But just tell me, did you have a good time?"

"The best! Fliss, I met this gorgeous man, he actually lives just a few blocks from here and—oh, I could go on and on about him, but…listen, call me soon, and if you need anything, anything at all, please let me know. I'll drop whatever I'm doing and come right over!"

After hanging up, Felicity crossed to the patio doors to check on Mandy. For a second she didn't see her and then alarm sent adrenaline coursing through her when she spotted the child. She was on the ladder, and stuck, very precariously, three-quarter-way up. The ladder swayed.

"Help!" Mandy screamed. "Fizzy! Help!"

Felicity shot outside, her heart in her throat. "I'm

coming, hold tight!'' If Mandy slipped, if she fell, if the ladder fell, she could break her leg, her arm, her neck...

She raced across the patio but before she'd reached the lawn she saw a tall figure move swiftly toward the tree, from the direction of the garage.

Jordan.

She stumbled to a halt.

In a second, he was at the foot of the ladder, his arms raised to hoist Mandy down. Catching her around the waist, he said something that Felicity couldn't hear, and the child let go of the ladder and fell back into Jordan's embrace.

Twisting around, she clasped her arms around his neck and lifted her tear-stained face to his. ''Daddy, I got stuck! And I wasn't supposed to go *near* the ladder, Fizzy told me, but I wanted to get RJ, 'cos he's up there and—''

She stopped abruptly as a silver-white shape sprang down from above and RJ streaked off across the lawn.

With a gulping little giggle, she said, ''Well, I guess he's not up there any longer!''

Felicity waited for Jordan to drop Mandy to the ground. He didn't. Tucking her against him with her bottom resting on one of his forearms, he held her cosily and smiled down at her. ''Where *is* Fizzy, poppet?''

He was treating Mandy in the same way he'd always done, with tenderness and love. Felicity felt off balance...as off balance as Mandy must have felt as the ladder swayed. Was Jordan putting on an act...or...?

''I'm here,'' she said.

Slowly, he turned toward her.

When she saw the strained lines on his face, her heart bled for him. This had to have been the worst day of his life. But as well as the sorrow she felt on his behalf, she also felt sick with apprehension. He was treating Mandy no differently from before. What could she expect for herself?

"Ah." His tone was one of quiet pleasure. "There you are." And he walked toward her.

His eyes were warm with love, and Felicity wondered if she was dreaming. She'd been prepared for an outburst of rage and hostility. She hadn't *dared* to hope for anything else. *Was* he putting on an act? But if so, why?

"I thought you'd be back earlier," was all she could think of to say.

His eyes never leaving her, he told her he'd accompanied the McTaggarts on the ferry and then driven them to the ranch. "Then there was a long wait to get on a ferry, and the ferry trip itself."

She said the first thing that came into her head. "That must have been frustrating." Her voice sounded as if it had come from far away; she barely recognized it.

"No. It gave me time alone. Time to think."

"Daddy." Mandy tugged his hair. "Can I get down now?"

"Sure. But first..." He whispered something in her ear and she turned to look at Felicity.

"I'm sorry," she said, "for going on the ladder. From now on, I'll do everything I'm told."

She tilted her head as Jordan whispered something else.

"Because," she said to Felicity, "if anything happened to me it would break your heart and it would break Daddy's too 'cos you both love me so much."

She paused as Jordan whispered some more to her.

"And most importantly of all, I have to not have any accidents so I can be flowergirl at your wedding!"

She turned innocent eyes to Jordan. "Is that all, Daddy? Did I say it right?"

Jordan hugged her and gave her a kiss. "You said it perfectly. Now—" he slid her to the ground "—you go and play with RJ. I have some things I want to say to Fizzy."

Felicity was standing in a daze. Was she dreaming? Why was Jordan looking at her like that, as if he wanted nothing more than to take her in his arms—

He took her in his arms. And she felt him tremble, just as her heart was trembling.

"I'm so sorry, darling," he said. "I should never have rushed away like that this morning. It was selfish of me to take off, leaving you to think God knows what."

"I understand." She wasn't sure how she managed to blurt the words out. "You must have been devastated."

"Yeah, shattered for sure. But that didn't excuse me from taking my anger out on you, you were just the messenger. And when I think how you must have dreaded the task—"

"Oh, I did, Jordan. I've been putting it off for so long, but...then Mom gave me an ultimatum. If I didn't tell you, she would. And then when you took off...I wasn't sure you'd come back. At least, not while Mandy and I were still here. I thought you'd be so furious and so hostile you might not want to see either of us again!"

"Darling, I didn't know what I was doing. I think, if I'd had Denny there at that moment, I'd have—well, I'm sure you can imagine what I'd have done to him. But my outrage was never at you or—God forbid—at Mandy."

Felicity hardly dared breathe. "So…you don't look at her in a…different way now?"

"Oh, I *do* see her in a different way now. Though I felt blindsided by what Denny and Marla did, I can forgive them for everything they did because I *owe* them. For *Mandy*. Ever since her birth, she's brought only joy to my life. I couldn't love her more if…" He laughed ruefully. "I was going to say 'if she were my own'. But dammit, she *is* my own! And she's dearer to me than anyone could possibly imagine. I see her now as a very special gift, Felicity, and one that came to me in a roundabout way, and that's the reason I see her differently. The only reason. I've loved her since the moment I set eyes on her, and I'll love her till the day I die." He shook his head. "When I think of how often I challenged you when you claimed you loved Mandy as much as if she were your own. Can you ever forgive me for being such a pompous dogmatic narrow-minded fool?"

Tears pricked Felicity's eyes. "Oh, Jordan, I can't tell you how happy you've made me. I was so afraid…afraid that after seeing the DNA results you'd no longer be *able* to think of yourself as Mandy's father."

"Ah, sweetheart." He gently brushed back an errant strand of her silky hair. "It takes more than DNA to define a Dad. Denny provided the sperm, and that's a biological fact. But *I'm* the one who was present at Mandy's birth, *I'm* the one whose name is on her birth certificate, and *I'm* the one who burped her, changed her diaper, sat up nights with her when she was sick. I'm the one who read her her first fairy tale, the one who showed her her first star, the one who cheered her on when she took her first step. *These* are the things that make a Dad, my darling…at least, any Dad worthy of the name.''

Felicity wondered if she'd ever been happier.

Jordan's eyes were glistening with emotion, and when he drew her close and kissed her, she felt the salt of tears on his lips. They could have come from her eyes or from his. But probably, she thought, they were a mixture of both.

''So,'' he murmured against her cheek. ''Shall we call my future mother-in-law and tell her there's going to be a wedding and Mandy's going to be part of her family for ever—though not in quite the way she imagined?''

''Oh, yes, my darling. Let's do that! She'll be over-the-moon, and happy that Mandy's got the two parents she loves.''

He put his arm around her and they walked to the patio, where Mandy was playing with RJ.

''Where are you going?'' she asked.

Jordan scooped her up and set her high on his shoulders. ''We're going inside to make a phone call.''

''Who're you gonna call?

''Your grandma.''

''I don't *have* a grandma!''

Jordan chuckled and his eyes met Felicity's. ''You do now,'' he said.

''Can I talk to her?'' Mandy asked eagerly.

''She would like that,'' Felicity said. ''She would like it a lot.''

So they all went inside. RJ padded in, too, right behind them…although because Jordan was gazing so besottedly at his two best girls he didn't notice RJ till the very last moment, and the poor cat almost got his tail snipped off by the door.

Harlequin Presents®
and
Harlequin Romance®
have come together to celebrate a year of royalty

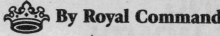 **By Royal Command**

EMOTIONALLY EXHILARATING!

Coming in June 2002

His Majesty's Marriage, #3703
Two original short stories by Lucy Gordan and Rebecca Winters

On-sale July 2002

The Prince's Proposal, #3709
by Sophie Weston

Seduction and Passion Guaranteed!

Coming in August 2002

Society Weddings, #2268
Two original short stories by Sharon Kendrick and Kate Walker

On-sale September 2002

The Prince's Pleasure, #2274
by Robyn Donald

**Escape into the exclusive world of royalty with
our royally themed books**

Available wherever Harlequin books are sold.

Makes any time special ®

COMING
NEXT MONTH...

An exciting way to **save**
on the purchase of
Harlequin Romance® books!

Details to follow in July and August
Harlequin Romance books.

DON'T MISS IT!

HARLEQUIN®
Romance®

EMOTIONALLY EXHILARATING!